HOLIDAY WATERS

HOLIDAY WATERS

CALL OF THE OCEAN, BOOK FIVE

by

GINNA MORAN

SUNNY PALMS PRESS

ISBN 978-1-942073-78-9 (soft cover)

Cover design by Silver Starlight Designs
Cover images copyright Depositphotos

For Inquiries Contact:
Sunny Palms Press
9663 Santa Monica Blvd Suite 1158
Beverly Hills, CA 90210, USA
www.sunnypalmspress.com
www.GinnaMoran.com

For Sarah and Katie

BREATHING AIR

BRIGHT AFTERNOON SUNSHINE BEAMS in through the balcony door of the captain's suite aboard the Ocean's King, haloing Ryan in warm light. He twirls his hand at me, motioning me to hurry and hang up the satellite phone.

I stick my tongue out at him. "That sounds perfect, Ava. Are you sure everything else is handled? Ryan and I can come help."

"I'm good. It's my year to prepare, remember? Giselle's a pro at parties, even underwater. Relax and enjoy the next few days. Use them to prepare for the ceremony." Wind whistles over Ava's soft voice through the line.

"Maybe you should do it alone again," I murmur. "I'm not as good as you yet. With the pirates and having to remain on the surface, I haven't had much—"

"You're going to do great. The colonies miss you and want to see your incredible magic in action. And if you need help, I'm here. We're in this together, remember."

"Listen to your queen, Luna," Ryan whispers, drawing my attention from the line. "Everything is fine."

"He's right," Ava says. "Just enjoy some time with your mate. Make some new traditions. Show your pirates what the holidays are about. And if you don't want that, then come dive down, but you're banned from helping. I command you to let us handle it for you."

I sigh. "But Ava—"

"I'll see you soon, okay? Wind's picking up and the *Wave Crasher* wants to pull anchor, so I have to go."

"Wait, I—" The line disconnects leaving me frowning. The vessel she boarded shouldn't be pulling anchor, and I know she said it to get off the line before I can argue some more. But I can't help it. I feel like I should be doing more to help our colonies prepare for the holiday festivities.

Ryan's form blocks out the sun completely as he closes the distance between us. He eases the phone from my death grip and pulls my hand up to his bare chest, drawing my fingers lower to his stomach.

"I know what you're doing," I say, taking over to explore his twitching muscles without his help. "And it's working."

He chuckles and plops onto the bed next to me. "You heard Ava. You're supposed to enjoy some time with me."

Sinking into him, I brush my lips to his, speeding up the beating of both our hearts, our sparks battling to outshine the sun of this beautiful, balmy December day on the Pacific Ocean. The last few months have been an adjustment as we flip-flop between the pirate and merpeople life, mostly sticking to the surface to oversee the changes of the Reyes Fleet while helping my crew adapt. Apart from a couple of incidents where I had to drop a few people on the cove for some extra training in our ways, life has been amazing with Ryan.

I kiss him deeper, soaking in the love and desire constantly crashing from him to me through our eternal bond as mates. I never thought I could love him even more, but I do. Ryan reacts to my fingers trailing down his body in a way I know he likes and rolls on top of me, framing my head with his elbows. His lips travel from mine to work along my jaw and to my neck.

"I was thinking," I whisper, arching my body into his under the tingles blossoming through me.

"You want to go to Pearlestria," he says between his kisses along my bikini top line as he shifts it out of the way. He stops for a second to peek up at me to confirm he knows what's on my mind. Which he does. Ryan knows me as good as I know myself. "If we go, Ava said no helping."

I reach and cup his face. "That's fine. She didn't say I couldn't watch."

"I might have some other ideas in mind if we go." He grins at me, tugging the strings on my bikini bottoms. "Because I don't think we've had enough ocean time together."

I giggle, his lust increasing the intensity of mine. "So, you're okay with going early? I know the human holidays are coming too, and we should—"

"My dad doesn't celebrate. There's nothing a thief hates more than gift giving."

I grimace. "Maybe that will change." Like everything else that has been evolving among my fleet of misfit, yet hard working pirates.

"Maybe," he says. "But Pearlestria first. Then San Francisco...and then maybe back to sea?"

I lick my lips. I know Ryan desires to spend more time away from the surface and the pirates, and I had planned on taking him, but it seems something always comes up. "I'd like that."

He grins. "Really?"

I nod. "These pirates can manage."

"You're right. Their captain has taught them well," he

says, scooting up closer to kiss me. "And we're always a swim away."

Happiness washes through me as we make our first official decision about our lives that doesn't involve anyone but each other. And now I can't wait. All I want to do is drag Ryan to the balcony and jump overboard to take him to sea.

"Before you start drifting, we have to let the others know," he says.

I crinkle my nose. "Maybe we shouldn't. I have a feeling that when the captain's away, the pirates will play."

"I'm sure Tide will hang around."

I smile at his comment. The ocean's best messenger has remained on the surface with us because of my cousin Talia. He hasn't mentioned it to me personally, but I know when a merman has interest when I see it. I can't wait for him to finally summon his courage. He's been growing a friendship bond with Talia over the last few months, and I know Talia likes him more than that. But neither has made a move, and Ryan won't allow me to give either of them a push as they figure things out...most definitely and soon together.

"I know he will," I muse. "And then—"

A knock sounds on our door. "Dinner, you two," Talia says through the wood. "Something special. I wouldn't wait or you might miss out."

Ryan rolls off me and pulls me to my feet, helping me

dress though we could skip a meal. But I don't like to. Mealtime has always been my way of connecting with my crew. If there's one thing we have in common, it's that we love to eat.

Stopping Ryan at the door, I slide my arms around him and hug him for a moment. "So, we'll leave tonight?"

He nods. "This will be the best holiday ever."

"Luna, duck!"

Glass shatters over my head and cascades to the floor behind me. The sun reflects yellowish light over the pieces, shooting pretty starbursts across the ceiling. Setting my fork down, I take a deep breath and push to my feet. If it's not colorful, impressive language with my crew, it's roughhousing. A gruff holler rips through the air, and a buff pirate shoves another over the balcony railing toward the sea.

"Oh, Ocean. Come on." Flicking my hand out, I summon a wave to catch the man, not letting him sink under. He hovers in the wave, glaring at the back of the head of the hulking pirate—a man people call Brutus—who threw him overboard.

I sigh and stroll to the whiteboard Ryan hung on the wall for me and erase the number two from the line Talia created for me to fill in as a joke that I've decided to take seriously. Now the whiteboard reads, *It's been 0 days since someone was thrown overboard and saved by a mermaid princess.*

"Nice catch, captain. But he deserved it," Brutus says, cracking a smile to show off his bright white teeth. If I wasn't supposed to chide him, I'd smile back, because I'm proud he's maintaining good hygiene, which is number three of the rules my fleet must follow, insisted on by Talia.

One of my first orders as reigning pirate queen was that everyone saw a healer. My crew, while quite nervous about having to submerge underwater for an exam and proper care from the best healers in the world, did exceptionally well. I never knew how complicated the human world could be about basic needs, especially if someone isn't fully immersed in it like my outcasts of reformed criminals, those in search of belonging, and those who love the sea as much as me. They don't have a home on land, but I'm happy to provide one for them on the sea if they follow the mermaid way.

I sigh again, a little too late to Brutus's comment and clear my throat to deepen my voice. "And I suppose you deserve to clean up this mess, right? It's only fair."

He grimaces and crosses his arms. "That's what the—"

"Hey, asshole, you heard the captain," Hawk says from the end of our table, where I allow anyone to join me for a meal when I'm on board. "Clean that shit up."

I swivel in my seat to smirk at Hawk. His loyalty and desire to work hard to meet our goals make him an invaluable crewmember. Behind all the foul language and gruff, bearded exterior, lies a kind heart. "You know, it's always nice to help."

Brutus laughs, and Hawk groans. All I can do is roll my eyes at the two of them. This is what I call taming and training pirates, making little suggestions instead of commanding them with threats. Ryan says the crew feels guilty if they don't give in. I guess even the toughest pirate isn't immune to a mermaid's request, and I use it to my advantage. I'd rather stick to my own approach and set a good example.

And plus, I have Ryan's dad to be the bad guy when I need it. Wren controls with authoritative command while I take the gentler approach, and I'm happy that he was wrong about needing to always scare the crew. They much prefer my nicety now that they don't have to worry about people seeing it as a weakness.

They're not always the best behaved, and I still have a few troublemakers on my crew, but mostly, everyone pitches in and works hard under my reign. If only I could get them to hug instead of punch each other as a form of greeting. I'm working on it, though. Talia has trained half of our crew to high-five, but sometimes that leads to strong whacks, which isn't much better.

"You heard my sweet and stunning mate. Be thankful she doesn't send you back to the cove for another lesson on manners." A plate of cookies plops on the table in front of me, smelling of chocolate and vanilla. Ryan kisses my cheek, hugging me from behind for a moment before taking the seat next to me. He twists to glance behind us, seeing both Brutus and Hawk cleaning up the glass while Ali reaches out and helps Dirk from my frozen wave.

"I still might," I say, leaning in to meet Ryan's lips, his mouth as sweet as the cookie he holds up to feed me. "After the holidays, though."

Another plate plunks on the table across from me, and Talia sits down, gently kicking my foot under the table with a grin lighting up her beautifully fierce features. She wears a bandana over her black tresses and a chain around her neck with the heart-shaped sea glass pendant I made for her. "You need to work on the consequences, Luna. The crew loves going to the cove."

I smirk. "They really have taken to the mermaid life, haven't they?"

Hawk returns to his seat, and I offer him a cookie, which he plops in his mouth. "It's because you all love to share," he says while chewing.

"When you behave," I muse.

A whistle sounds through the air, drawing my attention from Hawk and the others. Ryan hops to his feet first, scooping up half of the cookies and leaving the rest for Talia and the others. I follow behind him to the elevator to take up to the sundeck to where Darren keeps watch over the seas.

Darren greets me with a frown instead of a smile, his graying brows lowering on his sun-weathered forehead from years of island living outside of civilization. Raising his hand, he points at the crystalline waters. "Tide's coming."

"Tide?" I shade my eyes with my hand to peer at the blurring form of the ocean's messenger and a fierce warrior of Pearlestria as he propels at top speed in our direction. "Oh, no."

"Something must've happened," Ryan says, thinking my same thoughts out loud. Because Tide was supposed to be with Wren on the *Hurricane.* The Hurricane, one of the many boats of my fleet, monitors the surface activity in and outside of the protection provided by the coast and the human authorities throughout all the seas. If Tide's here, it could only mean there was a problem since they weren't supposed to come back until later this evening.

Too anxious to wait for Tide's arrival, I climb the rungs of the railing and dive from the Ocean's King and into the calm seas. Ryan splashes next to me and shrugs from his board shorts to transform. I can't help myself from staring at his handsome naked body as his black scales sprout from his legs, his body rippling with his transformation. With all of our ocean swimming as merpeople lately, Ryan's gained great strength and muscles that nearly match the best warriors of the sea, and his body will continue to adapt the more time we spend underwater.

He catches me checking him out and swims around me so quickly that I get caught in his whirlpool and spin into his arms for a kiss. Running his hands down my body, he undresses me, sending heat through me that quickly morphs my nerves into desire that leaves my spark racing even more wildly. As much as I love him in his human form, seeing him as a merman always pokes at my very nature. I'll never take his every breath of the sea for granted. The ocean gave me a gift I'll cherish forever with Ryan as my official mate on land and in the sea, taking on all the forms we desire.

Spasms seize my muscles, and I arch my back, my body wanting to follow Ryan's lead. Holding my hands, he watches me transform before him, my silver scales scattering light across his black ones to enhance the deep green fractals of color on his fin. The water shifts around me as my body adjusts, the magic of the ocean coursing through the sea enveloping me in a hug of relief as comforting as Ryan's arms around me.

"Princess Luna!" Tide calls from a few hundred feet away, pulling me from my moment with Ryan. "Prince Ryan!"

I nearly forgot why I jumped from the sundeck into the sea. The second we hit the water, it's easy to forget that the world spins outside us.

Ryan hooks his hands on my sides and jets us in Tide's

direction, still keeping his lips to mine for a moment longer. I snuggle against Ryan, appreciating his powerful fin, his fast swimming, how perfect my body molds to his, so it's like we're one being. Nothing in the world can compare to swimming like this with the merman who completes me. Unlike when he was human, Ryan no longer has to surface. We don't have to worry about air or depth. I've swum with other merpeople before, but swimming with my mate is something on another level, and I just love how well he's adapted from human to merman, never a doubt crossing my mind about how it's always supposed to be us and the sea, even if we help manage the surface.

"Has something happened, Tide?" Ryan asks for me, probably realizing how my heart drifts in the waves, and slows down as the sea's messenger comes up to us. He's longer than Ryan with a thick black beard that hides his mouth unless he smiles. And now, he looks like he might never smile again. I want nothing more than to swim back to the Ocean's King and ask Talia to join me, because I'm certain she might be the only one to make one of my oldest friend's happy.

Tide glances at the shadow of the Ocean's King behind us, and without having to ask, I know his heart wanders to Talia aboard for a second before his attention returns to us. I was right about who he needs to smile. "You must hurry. We have a problem."

And like that, a frown overtakes my expression. I was hoping he was just going to ask to come aboard because he couldn't wait until tonight to return. "What kind of problem?" I ask, searching Tide's face for an answer he's not quick to give. Whatever reason he's come seems to be worse than I thought. "I was hoping you were just going to ask to come aboard to share a meal with Talia."

He puffs a bubble through his lips and glances at the boat. "I want nothing more than my desire to spend time with the most enchanting woman I've ever seen to be the problem, but it's a pirate one, Princess Luna."

"Pirate? We are the pirates," Ryan says, fanning his caudal fin to keep us in place against the current Tide creates as he anxiously swims back and forth in the water.

"And we're the problem. It seems Wren has forgotten his way."

I grimace and let Ryan go to touch Tide's shoulder to get him to stop rocking the calm water. "I don't understand."

"Come on. I'll show you. But we must hurry. There are hostages involved. I wanted to take care of this for you with Winter Solstice coming, but I have no idea what to do." Tide grimaces, turning his attention back to the shadow of the boat shading the reef beneath us like he didn't want to have to give me this unsettling news. "I'm sorry."

My mouth drops open. "Wait, what? Hostages? Tid—"

He wrings his hands together. "Wren was adamant, and he is your chief mate, so I didn't want to act before consulting with you."

"Shit." Ryan accidentally projects the thought to me, his glittering green eyes lining with worry. Ryan's dad has been exceptionally well behaved the last few months, and I can't help wondering what went wrong today that set him back on a current I thought my ocean magic re-routed. He made a vow to the ocean and me, and I never imagined he'd break it. "This isn't good. Tide, take Luna with you. I'll catch up."

I nearly beg Ryan to stay with us, because I don't know how to handle his dad either apart from throwing him overboard or dropping him on an island, neither things I want to do.

Ryan doesn't give me the chance to plead with him and kisses me once. "I'll make sure to be there before you surface, okay? I'll handle him."

I release a relieved bubble. "And then I'm taking you to sea to make up for it."

He kisses me deeper. "Sounds like an amazing plan to me, because I plan to make it up to you too."

Ryan nudges me to Tide, who immediately takes my hand and propels us in the direction he came. My mate doesn't have to tell me for me to know that he's alerting the Ocean's King of what's going on so we have backup just in case. And maybe someone to take over, so we can head to sea before Wren can cause any more problems. But first, the poor hostages.

I knew I should've listened to Ryan. He warned me that it might be a bad idea to let his dad take another vessel unsupervised by us, even with Tide, because old pirate habits might be hard to break no matter how many weeks have passed. But I wanted to give the old pirate king the benefit of the doubt. I just don't understand what happened. And all before Winter Solstice, one of the most magical nights of the year and right before a trip I've yearned to take Ryan on that will keep us submerged while we really enjoy our lives together in the sea and plan our future as coupled mates.

And despite what Ava commanded, I should be helping with the holiday celebrations, or at least supervising, and for not only the one in Pearlestria but also Christmas on land for my human bonds. I much prefer party planning over dealing with pirate problems. I've spent so much time out of the water to get my crew to manage itself, and I can't help fearing that maybe it's our destiny to remain breathing air even after I finally managed to find balance and my place on the land and in the sea.

Tide picks up his pace, tugging me along until I finally draw my attention from my inner thoughts of all the plans Wren's stunt has immediately ruined. Ryan told me that neither his dad nor the crew celebrates the holidays, but Wren knew how important Winter Solstice was to us. It's my first one with Ryan. It's my first with Giselle as my warrior soul sister.

"It's going to be okay, Princess Luna," Tide says, glancing at me in his peripheral vision. "We still have time to get to Pearlestria. Try not to let this get you down. We'll get things worked out."

I puff out my bottom lip. "I hope so. I wanted this year to be perfect."

"Every year is perfect." He offers me a smile, squeezing my hand. "And I bet this year will be even better. You know, your cousin is looking forward to the celebrations as well. You are a lot alike."

His words bring a smile to my lips. "She's great, isn't she? I can't wait for you to finally ask her to court. You have been my friend forever, and I know it in my heart that she is your intended."

Blush sweeps across his cheeks. "I'm happy to hear you confirm what I feel in my heart, but I've learned the complexity of human bonds over the last year, and I want to assure I do this right."

"I'm sure you will."

Tide's admission about Talia distracts me enough to pull myself together instead of breaking under the pressure of my panic about my pirates. The world blurs as I flick my tail, getting used to swimming with Tide instead of being carried like Ryan prefers, his merman nature in full effect and comparable to other mated mermen in the sea.

Waving my fingers, I summon a current to help me maintain Tide's warrior pace so he doesn't have to drag me to the location of the Hurricane.

"So, how many hostages?" I ask Tide to break the silence falling between us as his mind surely drifts to Talia. "Anyone hurt?"

Tide glances at me in his peripheral vision, his smile disappearing with his tightening jaw. I'm sure he'd much prefer to talk about Talia instead of Wren, but I must prepare for the worst. "A crew of twelve on a fishing vessel. A few hostile. One injury."

I grimace. "How bad?"

"Wren refused my suggestion of a healer."

Shaking my head, I glare at the sea in front of us. Of course he did, and it doesn't surprise me one bit. I hate to think it, but at least it was Wren who was injured and not him injuring someone else. He's tough. He can handle it.

Tide slows our pace as we approach two boat silhouettes bobbing together on the surface. I catch sight of a discarded net blanketed across the ocean floor below and grimace at the sight of it littering my beautiful waters.

Breaking away from Tide, I dive down to retrieve the net, releasing a few creatures out from under it. Tide follows my lead and grabs the other end to fold it. He tucks it under his arm and heads to the surface, stopping to wait for me to transform.

"Shall we wait for Prince Ryan?" Tide asks, treading just below the Hurricane. Even though Ryan doesn't like being called prince, it's customary for warriors to do so with him as my mate, and merpeople love tradition, though it's one I'd love—and Ava would love—to break.

I flick my tail to break through the surface, just high enough to listen without anyone seeing me. I know if they do, Wren might put on an act or something to justify his actions. I just want to assess the situation the best I can before I decide what needs to be done.

"You're so damn lucky I don't feed you to the sh—" I sigh and sink under at Wren's threat. I wish he'd stop spreading lies about a shark's diet. He still doesn't understand that of course an apex predator will emerge when summoned with chum, but it doesn't mean it actually wants to eat whoever he thinks he can threaten this way.

"We should board now," I tell Tide. "Let me go first."

Closing my eyes, I will my transformation to take hold and then kick to the surface to clear my lungs of ocean water. Tide allows me to hold onto his shoulder while I shimmy back into my bikini bottoms. He follows my lead and dresses, and together we splash toward the stern of the Hurricane.

"So what we're going to do is—"

"Wren!" I yell, finding my footing on the deck. "What is going on?"

I stand in shock, peering around at the dozen men Wren has bound, sitting along the perimeter of the deck. Tide drips water beside me and drops the net he's been holding at his feet. The air reeks like it used to aboard the Ocean's King with the smells of pirates, but I know the assault on my poor enhanced out-of-water senses doesn't come from Wren or Gopi. It comes from the fishermen gaping at me like I emerged from the sea in my mermaid form.

Wren points at the men. "Eyes on the deck, and not another damn word. Got it? I don't like the way you're looking at my kid."

I close the distance with Tide right behind me. "Hostages, really? We talked about this." On more than a dozen occasions to be exact.

Wren glances at Tide and then meets me with a raised brow. "Hostages? No. This is a present for you, princess. I caught these guys doing...something that would hurt your pure mermaid heart and put a stop to it. I think we could use these assholes on our crew. They have skills but need direction. Merry Winter Solstice, Luna. It's great, right?"

Oh, Ocean. This was not on the wish list Wren demanded I give him because he said shopping for a mermaid princess was harder than taming a Great White.

I gape at him for a second before averting my gaze to the men and then to their boat anchored and tied to the Hurricane. The smell I caught a whiff of doesn't come from only the men but also from their entire vessel. And I take Wren's word for it, not needing to see whatever he put a stop to. But hostages? Not exactly what I'd call an acceptable Winter Solstice gift.

Water splashes behind me, and I feel Ryan's worry turn into annoyance through our bond. He had intended to catch up and board first to deal with this, but I couldn't help myself. Strolling over to me, he whispers an apology into my ear and then turns to Wren and says, "You couldn't get Luna something she actually likes, Dad?" He must've heard his dad before boarding. "I mean, seriously. I know you don't celebrate the holidays, but you promised you'd try for her, and this isn't trying hard enough."

Wren rolls his eyes, a gesture I'm pretty sure he adapted from me. "Don't worry, kid. I got her something else, too. But this was a must. Look in their boat, Ry, and tell me you wouldn't have done the same."

Ryan groans behind me, and I start to step toward the side of the boat, but hands lock around my waist, and Ryan hugs me from behind. "He's right. These aren't hostages. They're criminals."

"So what do you want me to do, captain? Cut them loose? Feed them to something hungry? Turn them into passable crewmembers? You know I can." Wren wags his eyebrows at me. "You know how much I like doing that. We'll call it a shared present. I get my fun. You get more good crew."

Sucking in a deep breath, I look at the men, panic crossing their faces. "I want you to go back to the Ocean's King."

Wren grumbles, tipping his head back to look at the sky. "That's not an option. You might need my help."

I shake my head. "We'll get this under control. Thanks for the present."

He frowns, concern pinching his brows together. "But you have to get ready for your—"

"Tide, take Wren and the fishing vessel. Tell the others that there has been a slight change of plans, and that we might not make it to Pearlestria." I turn to Ryan. "I'm sorry. I know you wanted to start our ocean adventure, but I can't just leave them."

If there was a contest for pouty mates, Ryan would win, and I feel terrible.

He quickly presses his lips together to smooth out his frown and takes my hand, bringing it to his cheek. "I guess I can enjoy a couple more hot showers with you."

"And blanket forts," I murmur.

"Luna, Ryan, I think that—"

I wave at Tide, and he grabs Wren and dives him over the side of the boat with him even though they could've just boarded the other vessel by stepping onto it. I hide my smirk with a smile at Tide's actions, knowing how Wren hates getting his boots wet or surprise trips overboard.

I turn my gaze away from Wren and Tide and draw my attention to the fishermen without a word.

"What are you gonna do with us?" a man asks despite Wren's instructions to remain quiet with their eyes on the deck.

Placing my hands on my hips, I meet his watery gaze. "I'm going to take you somewhere you'll learn the true laws of the seas. Plus, I think I could really use a vacation."

WORST GIFT EVER

THE SUN SETS THE ocean in the horizon aglow like a sparkling blanket of blue-gray that goes on forever. Ryan helps the last man ashore from the inflatable tender boat and motions for him to take a seat in the powdery sand under the shade of the tall palm trees.

I point at the ocean beyond the bay of Celestiana Cove. "You see that reef out there? Don't try to cross it. I'm not in the mood to send my mate on a rescue mission if any of you are brave enough to attempt to leave the island. These waters belong to us, and we don't take kindly to your blatant abuse of not only human laws but also the laws of the sea."

"What the hell is this place?" a man with a long white beard asks, peering in the direction of the small beach community a few hundred feet away. I'd have taken these men to the other side of the island, but I promised my dad I wouldn't drop people off without warning.

I thought him despising pirates was bad, but it doesn't compare to the hatred he carries toward anyone who dares attempt to venture outside the coasts of human authority on fishing vessels clearly not looking for a food source but only seeking to wreak havoc on our waters—and not against humans like pirates.

I shudder and push the thought away. "Welcome to Celestiana Cove, your first stop in the mermaid ways rehabilitation program. You've been found guilty of breaking several dozen ocean laws by my chief mate. Because it's the holiday season, you'll be staying here a few extra days under my care until my crew gathers and then you'll be dispersed to work among my ships." Because Celestiana Cove isn't an island prison anymore but a haven for people to adjust—merpeople and humans alike.

Whispers break out between them, and I hear a few ask each other what they think I meant by mermaids. Of course none of them will believe a word I say until they have concrete proof—me in a tail before them—but that'll come in time.

Now, I just want to get these men situated with an island host and head out for a real swim with my mate that doesn't involve receiving strange gifts from his dad.

"What?" another man says, speaking up from the commotion the rest of the crew makes. "Work for you? I don't work for—"

Ryan strolls away from me to tower over the scruffy-faced guy now flinching back under the intensity of my mate's heated gaze. His ability to adapt to any situation—from fierce warrior to blushing lover—never ceases to amaze me. "You must be the captain."

The man doesn't respond.

"I know your type," Ryan says. "And yes, you will be joining our crew. Because if you don't, there are far worse consequences. The sea doesn't take kindly to your kind of fishing adventures."

"What are you, environmental pirates or some shit?" he mutters. "You two are barely adults. How the hell did you find yourselves doing this?" His curiosity gets the best of him, opening him back up for a conversation instead of a staring match that could possible lead to me summoning the sea to calm everyone down.

I lift and drop my shoulders. "You can say that."

"Come on. There are bigger threats out there you should be worried about."

Ryan crosses his arms over his chest, turning to look at me. I nod my head to let him continue. "Everything adds up for us. If you willingly agree to consider yourself an ally to the ocean, you'll be rewarded."

"And if we don't?" the man says, his deep voice rising with his annoyance.

"You'll never travel the seas again."

The man glares at me, squaring his shoulders. "I'd like to see you try. You're outnumbered, you know. Are you sure you want to start a fight you can't win? Give us your boat, and we'll leave you peacefully. If you don't, well, you'll have a problem."

All the men start getting to their feet, scowls directed at Ryan over me. I take an automatic step back, pulling my mate with me to where I feel safest. He doesn't resist and lets me drag him into the rolling waves. His amusement washes over me, suppressing my nerves. He clearly likes my protectiveness over him.

"Please, calm down," I say, sliding in front of Ryan.

The captain strolls closer, balling his hands into fists. "Calm down? You stole our boat. You interrupted our operation."

I heave a sigh. Usually, we mess with lines and create rocky currents to stop vessels from testing their power on the sea. It's what Wren should've had Tide do instead of seizing their boat and handing the crew over to me like I'd appreciate more people to train. His present comes with a ton of work, and all I wanted was a vacation with my mate as merpeople and not as pirates.

If I wasn't on a mission to try to promote kindness with my own kindness, I'd have said something. I mean, it hurts my spark that I wish I had rejected a gift. I love gifts. Mostly giving them, but—

"You have five seconds to chill out," Ryan says, pulling me back into the safety of the bay.

"Or what?" another man asks, summoning his bravery from his crewmates.

"The sea will silence you," I say. I stand firm in place against the swells rising around us. Channeling my best Wren impression, I glower, daring the crew even to step closer. All it would take was for me to swing my hands up to send the waves crashing toward them, but something like that could cause injuries, and I'm not as great freezing the ocean, especially when I'm worked up. I doubt Ryan wants to fish fishermen out of the sea, and I know he would prefer if I didn't help.

The captain laughs at my attempt to intimidate him.

I don't react or let it get to me. I know what I'm capable of, and I don't need the cocky man to shake or cower. What I need is for him to stop trying to start things. Neither Ryan nor

I want to fight. We *won't* fight.

Closing my eyes, I summon a towering wave behind us, sending blue light sparkling across the cream-colored sand. Silence falls upon the crew, and a few of the men run back toward the tree line.

"What the—"

The wave crests, washing over all of us. I didn't mean to lose control. All I wanted was to get the fishermen to do what Ryan asked and to relax and take a breath. Ryan holds me, swimming us deeper into the bay where I can transform into my mermaid self. I find it easier to give in to my ocean magic in my true form. Revealing myself also helps me prove my point.

Ryan doesn't follow my lead, remaining human to prop me up on his shoulder as the waves settle and return to their constant roll forward and drag back motion of the magical tide. And I let him show me off, feeling his love and pride in carrying me out of the water wash through me.

His whole face lights up with a smile despite having to deal with these pesky fishermen. I could sink in every emotion he brings out in me. I don't have to be perfect at controlling ocean magic or even good at taming unruly humans. All I have to be is me. I smile wider at him, wishing he'd carry me deeper into the water instead of into the sand.

"You're way too excited," I whisper, rubbing my hand on

his shoulder.

"I can't help it. I love showing you off. I'm the luckiest merman in all the seas to have you as my mate." His words fill me up with everything good he summons inside me. Stretching his neck, he motions in the direction of the beach with his chin. "I mean, look at all their faces. They now see just how magical you are."

All twelve of the fishermen sit in the sand, now wet and disheveled and in utter shock as they stare at my silver tail sparkling like a diamond in the sunlight. Stars of light dance across the sand, and an older man shields his eyes from me. Ryan trudges closer, his chest puffing out, his arm muscles flexing as he steadies me.

"Are we dead?" a man asks his captain, rubbing the heels of his hands into his eyes. His gaping mouth reveals his yellowing teeth, and his dark eyes dart around, only peeking at me almost like he's afraid.

I laugh at his question, my voice echoing over the hum of the waves. I still find it amusing how humans always think they're dead if they see something they have trouble believing. "Most definitely not. You probably have a lot of questions, though. I want you to know that we're not going to hurt you, so please, don't fight anymore. I hate having to use the sea in such a way."

"Who are you?" the man asks, finally summoning the

courage to talk to me directly instead of to his captain. I'm glad he doesn't ask what I am, because I thought the tail was obvious.

"I'm Luna Torres-Lazaro-Reyes, princess of Pearlestria and captain and queen of the Reyes Empire," I say, smiling.

Ryan chuckles at the fact that I use all of my names when I introduce myself to people. I can't help it. I love them all, and there was no way I was giving any of them up. Each one makes up a part of me that I will cherish forever.

"You can just call me Ryan," my mate says. "Only our colonies use the title of prince to address me."

The captain sneers, shoving his hands into the sand like if he doesn't, he'll try to use them against us. "I don't care what anyone calls you. What I want to know is why you possibly think we would ever work for you? I don't work for no one but myself."

"It doesn't matter," Ryan says.

I nod, agreeing with Ryan. Because I can't truly explain why Wren would bestow a boat of fishermen on me right before Winter Solstice. I can't give a reason that would satisfy their curiosity. To be honest, I dislike the captain already and would prefer the alternative. "It's either this or land living. But not here. This island is ours."

"Or we could let the ocean decide," Ryan muses, sneaking in a phony threat. Unlike me, Ryan isn't entirely against using the old pirate ways to get someone to comply. But only with the mean ones I don't like to deal with. With Ryan, his threats come unfounded. I can't say the same about Wren.

I fake glare at my mate. Behind his tight jaw I know lies a smile he wants to give me with everything in his spark, but he won't tease and joke around in front of people who could possibly cause a whole lot more trouble for us than they already have.

"I have no qualms against setting you adrift to fight the sea for yourself," Ryan adds for good measure. "And these are magic waters. I can guarantee you will never make it back to civilization."

I ruffle Ryan's hair and smirk. "That's not necessary. I think we can work something out."

The men all look at each other, and then the old man with the long beard gets to his feet. Ryan stands tall in his place, not backing away as the man approaches. He extends his arm up to me but doesn't touch my tail. I realize he wants to shake my hand.

"I appreciate you wanting to work something out. Thank you for your mercy," the old man says, gently clasping my hand in his. "I work hard. Follow orders. I know my way around a boat. Just don't send me back to land."

"Yeah, because you'd never see outside a cell again." A younger man rubs his chin and looks in my direction. "You sure you want old Gus? He's a wanted criminal. Makes me nervous even to have him around."

Gus turns and punches the younger man, knocking him back. He seems to know the pirate way already, which I can't tell is good or bad at this point. I hold my expression even, looking between the two, though all I can think about is how well Gus will fit in with the other misfits of my crew.

"Wanted for what?" Ryan asks, speaking up for me.

He hesitates, making Ryan stiffen. "Armed robbery," the man finally says. "But that was a long time ago, and I'm a changed man."

"And you will continue to change," I say.

He nods. "Just don't send me back."

"I hadn't planned on it. Apparently my chief mate thinks we could use you and the rest of the crew to our benefit. And like I mentioned before, you're here for some mermaid rehabilitation. You'll be perfect for my crew when we're through."

The captain scowls, yanking the old man away from me. "What does that even mean?"

"It means be quiet and listen up," Ryan says. "Apparently my dad thought you were a good addition to our cause, and my incredible mate agrees."

Turning from us to his crew, the captain scowls. I half expect him to charge us, but all he does is swear. "I don't care about your cause. Come on, men. This is a load of shit. They can't just get away with—"

Gus swivels and clocks his captain in the jaw, knocking him back. Fighting breaks out among the men as they turn on each other. Ryan steps back and deeper into the water, shifting me off his shoulder and into his arms in case.

"We really need to work on Dad's gift-giving skills, huh?" Ryan asks me, smirking. His still light mood helps ease my annoyance. Obviously asking nicely for this crew to settle down and give us a chance isn't working.

"Or something. Because I'm pretty sure this might ruin Winter Solstice for us. You know we can't just leave them here, Ryan." I flick my hand out and send another wave crashing to shore to break up the brawling between the captain and Gus. "They'll get themselves hurt or hurt each other."

He stares at me a long moment, sucking his top lip between his teeth in thought. "I will absolutely not let this ruin such a special holiday for us, especially because I've never gotten to celebrate before."

"But we have to be in the sea for Winter Solstice," I murmur. "Not to mention Christmas in San Francisco. I promised Talia. We invited all our land family." It'll be the first time everyone gets to see the remodel of the magnificent house my mom left for me in Sausalito right on the San Francisco Bay and big enough to house many pods who want to try to explore human civilization away from the island.

"We'll make it work," Ryan says, keeping his eyes on the rowdy fishermen.

"I don't know if we can."

He snuggles his face into my neck. "You're pure magic. And you know what helps make the holidays?"

"Magic," I say, smirking.

"Now, calm those guys down enough so that we can separate them. And then we'll figure out Winter Solstice and Christmas."

I nod, sending the waves crashing over the disgruntled fishermen one more time. Dipping back under, I transform into a human to stand by Ryan's side. He pulls a few of the fighting guys apart, and finally gets everyone to listen up. As some of them smile and some of them glare, I can't help but think that I might need more magic to handle all this with Ryan. I might need a holiday miracle.

"Are you sure you want to handle it? I didn't mean to bring so many visitors, but my dad didn't give us a choice," Ryan says, linking his hands behind his head to glance at the twelve fishermen calmly sitting around a fire pit, shoveling food into their mouths. Right next to them, Blue and Sailor, two extremely intimidating warriors—Blue from my home colony of Pearlestria and Sailor from Reefaria—keep an eye on the crew while making them feel welcome.

"Of course I want to handle it. I've been welcoming people to this island for over twenty years. I've got it covered." Sandra strolls up beside Ryan to bump him with her hip. "I mean, look at them. A peaceful bunch when you feed and provide dry clothes to them."

"And summon tidal waves," I murmur.

Ryan presses his lips together, knowing well enough that I'm not happy about having to use fear to get the crew to finally stop fighting. "That does help."

Sandra reaches out and takes my hand. "I'm certain you won't have to do it again, Luna. Now stop worrying and enjoy your night here. I'll get everyone settled into the guest cabins, and we can figure things out come morning. You might even be safe to leave them with me."

"But my warriors will have to return to sea. You and twelve dangerous fishermen—"

Before I can finish my argument, Ryan spins and lifts me off my feet. I automatically curl my legs around his waist and giggle into his neck, kissing him a dozen times. Sandra shoos us away, scheming with Ryan to distract me from the unwanted Winter Solstice gift from Wren. After thanking Sandra again, we stop by the circle of people to tell the fishermen we'll see them in the morning. Sailor and Blue promise to summon us if we're needed.

A burst of laughter sounds out from down the beach,

drawing our attention from the group. Ryan sets me on my feet, and I dash ahead of him, daring him to catch me by wiggling my fingers for him to try. Another peal of laughter lifts my heart at the familiar voices growing louder over the waves.

"Gi!" I yell, kicking up sand as my best friend and warrior princess soul sister, as she likes to refer to herself as, pushes to her feet in the surf. "What are you doing here? Ava said you were sea deep in party planning."

"I had Tide send a message to Pearlestria for reinforcements here," Talia says from the ocean's messenger's broad back. She waves her hand at me over his shoulder. "I couldn't believe Wren thought this would be a good idea or a proper Winter Solstice gift."

"At least he tried, I suppose," I say, holding my arms out. "He's a work in progress."

"And should try harder. I told him as much, but he still thinks his gift of adding people to our crew was the best one you'd ever receive." Talia drops to her feet from Tide and kicks the rest of the way through the wet sand to me.

"That's yet to be determined, but he did what he thought was right. I trust his judgment. If he thought these fishermen would be more useful on our side rather than constantly causing damage to our sea, then so be it," I say, surprised by my own words.

"Ugh, Luna. You are way too nice. I would've made him

do all the work. I mean, Winter Solstice is only two days away and Christmas is next week," Giselle says, frowning. "He's stealing your holiday cheer. I can feel it."

"Well, he is a thief," Talia says.

"A reformed one, Lia," Tide says, calling Talia a name I've never heard anyone use. And I love it. Not because I think it's prettier than her full name, but because her smile widens under his comment, and I can't help myself from smiling. Tide will summon the courage to ask Talia to court him any day now. I can feel it stronger than ever, especially after our last conversation.

She reaches up and touches his cheek, sending my heart fluttering wildly. The excitement I feel in watching two souls fall in love is a present in itself and nearly makes up for the Wren mess because I have the opportunity to savor it since Tide will stay emerged when he usually treads the surface, only breathing air when he is called.

"I suppose you're right." Talia leans closer to him like she can't help herself, and he cups his own hand over hers.

Giselle giggles from her place next to Sun, and they smile at each other before she grins at me. I can see that Giselle finally understands the deep-seated instinct every mermaid has inside her that tells her when a merman is no longer available. She'll never admit it, but she loves this instant as much as I do. It's written all over the bond we share, our sweet emotions knocking back and forth between us.

"Whoa," she says, laughing louder. "This is so w—" Sun scoops her off her feet and dangles her over his shoulder, spinning her around. He knew she was going to blatantly mention something in front of Talia and did what any courting merman would do in the sea and help a merman out by making sure Tide gets to approach Talia when he's ready.

"If you'll excuse us, Princess Luna, Prince Ryan. I must take my mate to clean up in a hot shower before hunting for something to eat," Sun says, making Giselle laugh again as he takes off.

Talia crinkles her nose at me. "Please tell me you can shut off her emotions now."

I shrug. "Depends. I'm used to it though."

Ryan holds me close. "I make a pretty good distraction from them."

I giggle. "You both sometimes drive me a little nuts...but I'd never complain. It's interesting."

"Now I think I'm going to need a distraction from the lot of you," Talia says, eyeing Tide. His bright smile cracks through his neatly trimmed beard, his rugged, handsome face something Talia told me she enjoyed looking at.

It takes everything in me not to react. I don't even think she realizes that she's focused on him, but Tide is super aware. He straightens his shoulders and positions himself just right to give her the best view of him possible. Ryan squeezes my hand to get me to snap my mouth shut before I release a sigh. Oh, Ocean. Love never gets old, no matter who is falling for it.

"We were just about to swim to the other side of the island to visit with my dad and Dara," I say, my voice coming out higher in tone than I usually allow. "Would that be enough of a distraction?"

Talia lifts her brows. "I'll pass today. Even though punching your dad brings me great cheer, I'm a bit hungry and tired." Turning to Tide, she asks, "Are you staying ashore? How about I make us dinner? You know, as a thanks for the swim here? I know it must be torturous having to surface so much."

Tide takes her hand. "Far from it. It brings my spark great pleasure to swim with an enchanting, fierce woman such as yourself. I'd remain on the surface if you asked me."

The look she gives him speaks volumes of the bond she's developed with him over the last few months. A breathless, uncontrollable coo escapes my lips. Both Talia and Tide turn away from each other, realizing that despite how they feel, they're not alone on this beach. Talia's cheeks burn with embarrassment, but Tide only grins even more, so proud of himself for capturing her attention.

"Okay, we're going to go now." Ryan tugs me away from Tide and Talia before I can inch closer and get more invested in their conversation with each other. Peering over his shoulder, he says, "You two have fun. Call for us if you need anything. Sandra's on fishermen watch with Sailor and Blue, so don't worry about them."

I wave and smile, twirling in a circle a few times to peek at my cousin in probably the most obvious way as she and Tide watch us go. Ryan chases me on the beach as I continue to playfully dance out of his reach, and I finally relent and let him pick me up. He runs with me into the waves, and we dive in together and meet for a kiss in the surf. I can hardly contain myself and kiss him deeper, running my hands up and down his body. Even though the day ended in a semi-disaster, the night's looking so much better.

"I was worried the holidays were ruined for you," he whispers, clutching me in the crashing waves. "You have no idea how happy I am to feel you bursting with excitement like this. I could survive on it forever."

I grin. "I can't help myself when it comes to mates. They are so cute. The holidays are the most popular time for such a thing in the colonies. The seas will flourish in no time."

He chuckles, shaking his head. "Is that so?"

I nod and waggle my eyebrows at him. "Can't you sense it? My instincts are going wild every time I see them together. Their coupling ceremony will be so amazing."

Shaking his head, he pulls me close and whispers. "How

about you let *Lia* and Tide have their first date before you start envisioning their future?"

I squeal, leaning back to shake his shoulders. "You caught that too? *Lia.* Lia!"

"You know, Giselle was right about something feeling weird. The moment Tide said her name like that was the moment something shifted."

"You mean?" I knew Giselle and I felt the shift in Tide, but Ryan confirming something being different about Talia proves it.

He kisses me. "It was like her interest in him was palpable."

"I'm sure we'll be welcoming Tide into our pod in no time," I say, squeeing again.

Cupping my cheeks in his hands, he kisses my giggles away until I gasp against his mouth, my excitement shifting hotter. "That's better," he murmurs. "I prefer it if you envision our future with those kinds of feelings."

I pull away and poke his nose. "You didn't think I excluded us from my idea of making the seas flourish, did you?" I tease, biting my lip between my teeth.

His cheeks flush with rosy warmth even under the silver moon as I prod at his very nature as a merman. I was worried Ryan wouldn't adapt as quickly from treading the surface so often, but his desires mirror mine. Unlike other human-born merpeople, Ryan's discarded his humanity to the waves.

"I was hoping you didn't after today. I'd send my dad to the middle of a continent if that was the case."

"Nothing could ever change my mind."

"Good, because I know your heart's into it with the accidental transformations I love to elicit from you."

It's my turn to blush. I can't deny how much my mermaid spark loves being with Ryan in our true forms. While inconvenient at the moments my body chooses to rebel, Ryan's flattered. He loves it as much as he loves me.

He kisses each of my flushed cheeks before my lips. "And I promise I won't let anyone or anything ruin our plans to see where the ocean takes us on this adventure."

Swimming me deeper into the water, Ryan tugs me away from shore. We stay in our human forms, treading water under the bright light of the moon. The glowing ocean glitters around us, and I scoop up water to freeze into an orb, reflecting the silvery light from above, turning it into what looks like a light bulb.

Ryan touches it, feeling my magic in his fingers before it breaks to plop into the sea. I dip under water and release a stream of bubbles in excitement, thinking about Ryan's words, about Talia and Tide, about everything I love about this time of year.

It takes Ryan pulling me back to the surface to calm

down, though I'm antsier than ever to swim.

I hug him again. "This is going to be the best Winter Solstice and Christmas—"

"And the holiday of thieves ever," Ryan finishes for me.

"Holiday of thieves?" I ask.

He shrugs, gracing me with the brilliant smile I love. "We might not have celebrated traditional holidays like land folks, but we had our ways."

My excitement blooms at just the thought of starting new traditions and building on the ones I can't wait to share with Ryan. "I want to celebrate all the holidays and traditions. Every way possible. And new ways with you. I don't care if we're stuck on this island."

Hugging me close, he nuzzles his nose to mine. "Then I'll let the ocean know. These are about to be holiday waters."

HOLIDAY WATERS

"MY DAUGHTER, WHAT A surprise." Dad meets me in the waves and engulfs me into a hug. He kisses each of my cheeks, smiling with happiness that adds to the warm and fuzzies that have been rolling through me from both Ryan and Giselle. I don't think they teamed up to blast all the negativity out of me, but whatever my pod's doing is working.

"We brought dinner," Ryan says, hoisting up the giant albacore nearly the size of me in my human form. He usually only catches fish half this size unless he's with other mermen, but he hunted the biggest one he could find outside the bay in the short period of time we had to impress my dad. "Hope you're hungry."

Dad laughs and smacks Ryan on the back. "My son, I haven't caught a fish that size since..." He shrugs without finishing his thoughts. We all know he's thinking about his time before being stripped of ocean magic and his merman form, but none of us have to remind him. "Thank you. I'm famished."

Dad takes the fish from Ryan, and we follow him to shore to the small cabin he built only a week after Ryan's grandma decided to stay instead of following us back to sea aboard the Ocean's King. While their companionship doesn't feel like those I know of between merpeople, I think they've grown fond of each other. Dara's the only one my dad likes around apart from me and Ryan. He'll occasionally tolerate Wren for Dara's sake, but Wren and my dad both butt heads even with their commonalities.

Dara appears in the doorway of the cabin and beams us a smile. Her long silver hair winds into an intricate braid decorated with strands of the pearls and shells my dad asked me to bring ashore. Wren nearly lost his cool that I gave away so many pearls deemed valuable in the human world, but there was no way I was going to deny my dad his need to give Dara something, proving he still follows the traditions of the sea even if he's bound to land.

"My grandbabes," Dara says, opening her arms wide. "We weren't expecting you for a few days."

Dad strolls up to Dara and shows off the fish Ryan hunted before leaning in to kiss her cheek to make his way inside. Ryan eyes me, and I smile. A strange wave of emotions trickles from him to me, making me raise my eyebrows. He's suddenly uncomfortable by the new affection my dad shows Dara.

I stand up on my tiptoes to whisper in his ear. "What's up?"

"You don't think their cohabitation is weird?" he asks, keeping his voice low. "I mean, he's your dad."

"And yours," I muse.

He deadpans. "Definitely not helping, Luna."

I laugh. "Is this about the age thing? You know age doesn't matter, and you're thinking like a human, Ryan. Dara will certainly keep Dad on his feet. I was worried about his age and how he'd fare since he's well past a human lifetime. I'm just happy they've found something in each other. It's good for them."

He slowly nods his head. "You're right. I'll get used to it."

"You better, Ry," Dara says from her place in the kitchen. "Because Attilonious created a good life here, and I'm going to continue enjoying it with him."

I grin at Dara as she smiles at my dad. Ryan only nods and turns his attention away from them while they prep the fish. Dad's gained some table manners in the last few months. I don't think I've seen him eat a fish like this in my life. Who knew it only took an old pirate healer to help him truly adapt as a human.

After our meal in which there wasn't any leftovers, Dara and Ryan stay inside to catch up on the pirate life. He still seeks guidance from her on keeping everyone, including Wren, in check. I love seeing them together, feeling their bond that now extends to me. I never knew what it was like to feel such a thing, but with Ryan came his familial bonds, and I'll never take any for granted...despite Wren's antics.

I follow Dad out onto the beach lit in moonlight. He strolls next to me into the waves a good ways down the beach, just soaking up the comfort my presence brings him. I used to only visit him in my mermaid form, but now that Ryan and I have coupled, I like to come to shore and connect with my dad on a more human level.

"So, tell me, Luna. How are things really? I see the beautiful smile lighting your face, but I know you well enough to see the dissatisfaction lingering in your eyes. You look exactly as I remember your mother."

I freeze in the sand, my heart picking up pace at the mention of my mom or the fact that he points out how I look like her now more than ever since I found my ocean magic, and it broke the magic my dad used on me to make us look alike when I was a merbabe so we could bond.

"I—" My lip quivers, the dam I built out of the love and happiness I see in others shattering. And then I start crying, tears splashing down my face. "It's nothing. I'm being selfish."

"Is this about the fishermen you brought to shore?" Dad asks, recalling our brief conversation of why we've come from the sea before Winter Solstice.

I shrug. "Partly. I mean, I should be grateful that Wren helped the ocean by putting a stop to these men's cruelty, but it's almost Winter Solstice and mine and Ryan's first together. I should be in Pearlestria helping Ava and getting ready for the moon ceremony. But I'm not even that good with my ocean magic. Everything keeps piling up, so I haven't even had a chance to work on it with her. Now I won't be able to. My heart just wants so badly to return to the water. It's a feeling I can't shake."

The words spill from my mouth like the high tide pouring down cliff rocks in a waterfall and back into the ocean. The second I say them out loud, they drift into the sea, causing a swell to rise on the beach. I don't even have a chance to react before it cascades over us and knocks us off our feet.

Dad hooks his arm around me and pulls me to the surface with him. He stares at me a long moment, just taking in the sight of my sopping hair that streams water onto my face to blend with my burning tears. "My daughter, there is nothing selfish about wanting to return to sea with your mate to help the colonies. You've done so well with the surface that it might be the perfect occasion to take some time to care for yourself and Ryan."

"We were planning to after the holidays, because my crew has been doing so well, but now I'm not sure." Another wave lifts us off our feet, and Dad holds my hands through the movement. "My pirates need me."

"And so do our people," Dad says. "They need to see how to balance the unity you and Ava created."

"I don't even know how to balance it all," I murmur.

"We start with your magic."

"But Ava—"

"Isn't the only one who understands ocean magic," Dad says, chuckling. "I might no longer possess such a gift, but I can still help you if you'd allow it. And stop worrying about the fishermen. If they're who hold you back from returning to sea, I'll step in your place and see to it that they are prepared to be your allies. My gift to you, daughter."

I blink a few times, more tears watering my eyes. "You'd do that? I know how much you dislike—"

Pulling me into his arms, he hugs me. "For you, I'll do anything. I might be bound to the land, but my heart will always drift to sea."

"Maybe just for the holidays. I really don't want to miss

them."

"Whenever you like," he says.

I grin and kiss his cheeks. Who knew a grouchy shunned king could bring me so much Winter Solstice cheer? Looks like I might have gotten my holiday miracle after all. And I won't take it for granted.

"Close your eyes," Dad says, standing behind me. "Don't watch the ocean. Feel it around you. Listen to the call."

I tread water in my mermaid form while dad floats on his back next to me, just drifting back and forth on the calm waters. Ryan and Dara sit in the sand, watching us, and it takes everything in me not to peek at Ryan for the millionth time, at how handsome he looks with the glow of the fire lighting up his defined muscles.

"Do you hear it?" Dad asks.

Shutting my eyes, I follow Dad's lead and lie on my back, slapping my caudal fin on the surface. The ocean hums in my ears, muting the whistling of the balmy breeze stirring up the salty scent of the water.

"Now imagine you're made purely of the sea. Project everything you feel inside you to the waves."

The water warms around us, surprising me. It's the first time I've raised the temperature on purpose. And despite trying to remain calm and soaking in all of Ryan's projected tranquility, the annoyance of thinking about Wren spills from me first.

"Now use that to lift us up," Dad says.

A swell rises beneath us, the ocean reacting to my desire to lift us. Creating waves and freezing the water is usually the extent of my ability.

Dad's fingers lace through mine. "Good. Now slowly lower us. Don't let the wave crest."

I attempt to do what he says but lose concentration for a split second. The water thrusts us forward, heading right toward the beach where Dara and Ryan watch. Panic washes through me. I hadn't realized how big the wave was until I opened my eyes. And now it's cresting.

"Luna!" Dad yells. "Freeze it!"

Jerking my hands out, I grab hold of the swell and squeeze my eyes shut, imagining the ocean listening to the panic in my heart. The wave freezes under my magic, the clear water glowing in the silver moonlight. Dad hollers and drops from the wave now casting blue shadows across Ryan and Dara's startled faces as I hover over them. I clench my jaw, reeling the wave back to sea before it wipes out all the hard work my dad put into building his cabin just down the beach.

But I'm not strong enough. I lose control over the wave, and it cascades down onto Ryan and Dara, and I lose sight of my dad in the sand. The water blurs around me with thousands of bubbles, the wave colliding with the shore and rushing all the way up to the tree line. It takes everything in me to swim in the hot current I created that now drags back to sea.

"Luna," Ryan calls to me telepathically, already in his merman form. "Where are you? Do you have your dad?"

Spinning in the water, I search the sea and realize I'm far past the reef that creates a barrier for the island, the magic surrounding it making it impossible for humans to find without the help of merpeople. Out here, the water settles, released from my magic current, but there isn't any sign of my dad.

"I'm in the open sea. Dad's not with me. Is Dara?"

"She's okay. I'm coming to you."

I don't even swim a few feet before Ryan jets up to me, the power of his fin creating a new current that pushes me a few feet away from him. He catches me in his arms, touching my face for a moment.

"Attilonious wasn't on shore. We have to find him," Ryan says.

I inhale a deep breath of water. "Oh, Ocean, Ryan. Do you think?"

He doesn't say anything. He doesn't have to.

The ocean washed my dad away. He's gone.

SPECIAL GIFTS

"DON'T PANIC. ATTILONIOUS IS a great swimmer," Ryan says. "And he can hold his breath longer than even we can in our human forms."

"What if I accidentally pushed him past the barrier? The ocean doesn't allow it. He tested it after our coupling to see if he could venture out again, but he couldn't. Sailor had to retrieve him. Our coupling was his one free pass," I murmur, remembering how angry I was that he would endanger his life without consulting with me first.

My magic gave him a pass on the most meaningful night

of my life, and it was only because the ocean allowed me and Ava to extend the barrier for the occasion. It wouldn't forget the years of imprisonment my father assured in his failed reign.

"He'll be okay," Ryan assures. "We just have to find him, but you have to calm the water. It's getting rough."

I groan, holding my hands up, willing the seas to settle. But the more the seconds tick by, the worse it gets. It's like not having my magic all over again with how the ocean responds to the fear gripping my heart, reacting to me instead of allowing me to control it.

Ryan closes the distance, pressing his taut body into me, his tail sliding against mine, sending tingles through me. Leaning in, he kisses me, holding me close. "I'm here, and I know you can do this. You're my amazing, powerful, magical, pirate princess mermaid mate. The ocean loves you as much as I do," he whispers.

I scrunch my face, squeezing my eyes shut. "I can't."

"You can. You will." Ryan rubs his hands up and down my back. "Because the second everything is settled, I'm going to carry you back to shore and really help you relax."

I release a breathless laugh. "Ryan."

The waves calm around us, and I can finally see through the churning bubbles glittering in the soft moonlight like millions of light bulbs scattered through the sea. Ryan jets me back and forth through the water along the reef with no sign of my dad.

I suppress my tears as much as I can, and we jet toward the shallows. "Oh, Ocean," I say for the hundredth time. "Please."

"Luna, Ry!" Dara yells from the beach. "Hurry. He's here."

I gasp a relieved breath and say another prayer to the sea for making sure Dad hadn't swept away into water where he's no longer welcome. Ryan swims under me, and I hook my fingers to his shoulders and hug him as he propels through the waves and right onto the beach a half a mile from where I was practicing magic with my dad.

"He must've hit his head on something," Dara says, motioning us closer. "He's bleeding."

I crawl closer, dragging my tail with me. Dad lies in the sand, blood staining its cream color. "Ryan, a healer. He needs a healer."

"I'll go get my kit. Stay with him," Dara says, hurrying to her feet. "Ry, put pressure on the wound."

Pulling my dad onto my lap, I cradle his head in my hands, touching my fingers around the gash caused by my inability to remain in control. "This is my fault."

Ryan shifts closer and holds his hand over the wound. "It's not. It was an accident. You know as well as I do that the sea does what it wants no matter how much magic you have."

A wave crashes over us, and I brace myself against Ryan's sturdy form. He uses his other hand to cover my dad's face and nose, stopping him from breathing water. Tears burn my eyes. Another swell collides over us, determined to submerge us and make things worse.

"Please," I whisper to the sea. "Don't do this."

"Control it," Ryan says, his voice deep and commanding. He almost sounds like Wren, though his demand only makes me want to try harder, unlike the old pirate king who annoys me more often than not.

Water cascades over us again, this time strong enough to drag us back. I dig into the sand with one hand and hook my fingers around Ryan to anchor myself to him. "Something's wrong. I can't stop it. It's like it wants us—"

"Whoa, shit," Ryan says, drawing my attention from the sea around us and back to him. "My hands feel weird. Do you see them?"

The wave pulls back into the ocean, leaving us again in the sand. I peer at Ryan's hands, not seeing anything out of the ordinary. His muscular arms flex as he adjusts his hold on my dad once more.

"What about them?" I ask.

His brows furrow as he studies his hands. "They were glowing."

"Glowing?" I ask. "The only time I've heard someone mention glowing hands was from a healer. And you're not a mermaid. Mermen don't get those kinds of abilities."

Another wave crashes over us, and Ryan swears through my mind. "You sure you don't see anything? It's only in the water."

I puff a breath of air through my lips and purposely pull a wave from the sea to curl over us. Ryan presses his hands to my dad's head, his whole face lighting in wonder. Dozens of bubbles cling to his skin, but the only light I see belongs to our sparks beating in perfect rhythm in our chests.

"What are you doing, Ry? Get him out of the waves," Dara calls, running in our direction.

"Summon one more, Luna," Ryan says. "I just—something's different. Trust me."

I shift, glancing between my dad and him. "I always trust you."

"Then summon one more."

Ignoring Dara's yells, I call the ocean to me, bringing a wave onto us. Ryan swears again, but not against the ocean. Excitement runs over me in a comforting rush that makes me smile despite my worry. The wave drags the sand beneath us back to sea, and Dara yells out again, closing the space between us. She pulls Dad off my lap, using the strength I've only seen in warriors, managing to get him to the sand.

Dara scowls as she runs her fingers through Dad's wild, wet hair to pull the salt and pepper strands from his face. "What were you thinking, you two?"

Ryan pulls himself closer and hovers over my dad, ignoring the heat of anger Dara aims directly at the both of us, reminding me of the fierce protectiveness mates carry for each other. She and my dad might not share a merpeople's bond as humans, but it feels comparable.

"I was thinking that I'm a healer," Ryan says, flipping his hands from front to back, gazing at his palms a moment like he can see something I can't.

I jerk my attention to him. "Ryan, I told you—"

"Well, shit. You do take after me," Dara says, shining a flashlight on Dad, lighting his face to get a better look at him.

Dad groans and blinks, sitting up on his elbows. Gasping, I throw myself forward and onto his chest. He wraps his arms around me, pulling me closer. A smile lights up his whole face as he looks between me and Ryan. And then I turn my attention to Ryan, my mouth open in astonishment. I can't believe what I just witnessed. Mermen don't get the same skills as mermaids. He shouldn't have been able to use ocean magic to heal my dad's wound. Only healers can. I can't even do it. I can control it and use the sea but not like a healer. But Ryan did. He staunched the bleeding without needing help from a human medical kit.

"Ryan, that was...incredible and confusing," I say.

Dad sits up on his elbows. "He used you and the sea. Healers can't control ocean magic, but they're gifted with feeling it, using it to care for our people." Looking at Ryan, he says, "It seems to be a familial trait. Apart from your grandmer, your mother was gifted with such an ability. What an honor, my son. The ocean bestowed upon you something I haven't seen a merman acquire in a long time."

"I didn't know it was possible," I say.

Dad reaches out and squeezes my shoulder. "Anything is possible, my daughter. And I believe this is another sign for you to head to sea."

I frown. "I don't know if it's a good time to do it now. I mean, I might mess everything up. Maybe this was a sign from the ocean. I should just stay. We can have our own Winter Solstice here as a pod."

He shakes his head. "No. I want you to go. I know your mind has always drifted to land, my daughter, but your heart belongs to the sea. You need it for your magic. You can still have the surface under control without being immersed in it. Just think about it. Don't ignore the feelings inside you. If you do, you'll lead yourself astray."

Ryan hugs me between my dad. "He's right, Luna. I can feel how much you want this. You, me, and the sea. The land. The surface. You know I'll follow you anywhere."

If only everything wasn't pulling me in all different directions.

Because right now? I have no idea where I'm supposed to go.

"I'll think about it after the holidays," I finally say. "I just want to get through them."

Ryan takes me from my dad's arms. "And enjoy them."

If only that were possible.

DRIFTING TO SEA

"STAY STILL," I WHISPER, brushing my lips to Ryan's collarbone. "I'm not through kissing every inch of you."

He chuckles and tugs me up until our lips meet. "I'm supposed to be the one helping you relax."

"Oh, you are."

He moans, reacting to the weight of my body. "I know you don't know what you want to do, but I'm pretty set on never leaving this blanket fort."

Trailing my hands lower, I continue to map Ryan's skin with my fingers until he intakes a sharp breath. He flips me off him and lies on top of me, kissing me deep enough that I curl my legs around him, just feeling the heat of his body pressing into mine.

He leans slightly away to meet my gaze. "Again?"

I respond by biting my bottom lip.

"All right. My mind is set." His desire cascades from him to me to set off my own lust to explode through me in delicious waves I'll happily sink into. "This is our life now."

I laugh, arching up to kiss his throat, gliding my hands around his waist to grab his cute butt to pull him closer. He moans into my hair, his voice vibrating through me as I devour his love and distraction. With Ryan, especially in moments like these, life doesn't seem so out of control. The simplicity of living and breathing and loving Ryan calms the restlessness inside me.

What I want from my life with Ryan has never been so clear. I want to continue to create a better world with him, and in doing so, we need to take a breath and jump from the surface and into the ocean.

My dad was right about my mind focusing on land while my heart drifts into the sea. It's my home, and the home I've always imagined with my mate, with Ryan. He should get to experience the life he desires as a merman. While he's happy with me regardless, I see how much he craves to explore the deep, to travel the world, to do something more than accept the pirate life—no matter if it has changed—to find some-thing of his own in our world. I want nothing more than to give it to him.

"Luna," Ryan whispers, smirking at me. "You're trans-forming. Guess we have to move."

Heat burns my cheeks at the sight of my pectoral fins jet-ting from my arms. This is the third time it's happened in a month that I triggered my transformation during a moment of passion with Ryan. I just can't help it for some reason no mat-ter how much I love being human on land.

"Oh, Ocean. Not again. I mean, seriously, body?" I'm more annoyed than embarrassed, especially because Ryan con-tinues to kiss me without stopping or freaking out. We both agree it's because of my deep-seated nature as a mermaid that I want to be in the sea with him especially after everything that happened with Giselle that made us think such a life together was impossible, but in this moment, I'm perfectly content on land in our blanket fort. I wish I could just stop it.

He runs his fingers over the silver scales sprouting over my hip as hard as I try to suppress it. "It's definitely serious."

Lifting me off the bed, he carries me toward the door with the blankets still around us, making me laugh.

"Ryan, what are you doing? I can hold off for you to get dressed." Something's different in this moment with him. And I like it. He usually rushes to get dressed because he still clings to certain human social norms but not tonight. He's calmer. In more control than me. I wasn't sure he'd ever be this way after I sunk a ship during a moon-forced transformation. Though my magic is in my control, it's still occasionally untamed, and Ryan makes it go wild.

"No way. You obviously want to be in the sea with me," he says, chuckling. "I'll be okay. It's different here than on the Ocean's King." He's right about that. Nudity is accepted among merpeople, and I'm rather excited about his admission. Not because he's breaking through his comfort zone but because he's accepting who he is.

Only hesitating a moment in the doorway of the cabin, Ryan rushes us toward the glowing waters under the still night sky, his human rationale suppressed by his merman nature, making him so incredibly hot. I loved Ryan as a human. I had accepted the possibility of a life with him human and me as a mermaid, but I'm so thankful we get this life together. He deserves such a life as amazing as he is.

"And I told you I'd follow you anywhere," he adds.

I laugh again as he drops the blanket on shore, kicking it with his foot but failing to save it from a cresting wave. Disregarding it to find later, he runs into the waves, never taking his mouth off mine until he dives us under together.

I expect Ryan to wait for me to finish transforming so I can change back, but he transforms right beside me, his smile lighting up the water as he takes me in. The glow of the setting moon illuminates his tan, pearlescent skin, shadowing his body in all the right places. His emerald eyes sparkle like the flecks of green color in his black tail. Just watching him watch me sends our hearts beating wildly.

Closing the distance first, I caress my lips to his, the oxygen still clinging to his mouth tingling against my skin. I give into the sea completely, my mermaid nature, loving how unfazed Ryan is by my weird and inconvenient transformations. He swims around to take in the view of all of me as a mermaid, making me feel so beautiful without him having to say the words.

Ryan hugs me close again, his body touching mine completely. He jets us away from the shallows and spins us a few times through the sea past the reef. Swimming us at his top speed, he navigates the water for me, never letting me even flick my tail. A dozen images pass from my mind to his, and he hums against my lips.

"Where are we going?" I ask through another kiss the farther we get from shore. "We can transform and head back to our blanket fort. I'm good now."

"It'll still be there when we return," he says, his voice light in my mind. "Like I said, you want to be with me in the ocean, so we're going to be in the ocean until you're truly ready to return to land."

I purse my lips. "But—"

He shakes his head, stopping my telepathic thought. "No arguing. I can feel how much you love this, and I have a surprise for you anyway. I was going to wait until Winter Solstice, but now is a better time than ever."

My heart picks up pace at his mention of a surprise. I flick my hand, creating a current that clears a path in front of us so Ryan doesn't have to dodge all the ocean animals that attempt to get in our way as they gravitate to me.

Ryan tightens his arms around me, his own satisfaction from swimming rushing through me. I listen to the thrum of his heart in my ear, feel the beat of it under my palm, and just soak in the moment. And I missed it more than I realized. It's not often we've gotten to just swim together for no reason apart from each other. The last time was on the full moon because pirates are needy. Protecting the ocean from the surface is a huge job, the only thing keeping it manageable is Wren's fierce reputation. But it's getting better now that we've united the land and sea. It won't be long until things get back on course.

Closing my eyes, I relax, enjoying our swim away from Celestiana Cove and my lingering worry about the fishermen, about my dad, about the holidays.

Ryan kisses me again and dives us together away from the surface and toward the sandy bottom. I don't have to look around to know that we're still pretty close to Celestiana Cove but far enough away that the ocean feels more private. We're not near any of the larger currents merpeople travel and still close enough to emerge from the deep.

The water shifts around us, calming completely along with my heart. My eyelids turn from dark to light like the sun rose, but I know dawn is still an hour away. I pull back from Ryan's kiss and open my eyes.

"What is this?" I ask, peering around the enclosed space.

Tipping my head back, I study the silver rocks glowing like the light of the full moon on the roof of the merperson house Ryan brought me to. He grins and sets me in the sand, flopping next to me but never taking his gaze from mine as I absorb the beauty of the decorated walls.

"Our home away from home, away from home, away from home," he says, running his hand across the sea floor. A few colorful fish dart out from a reef under the window cutout to play in the strands of my floating hair. "For when you need it to be just you, me, and the sea. No pirates. No royal duties. No land stuff. Just me."

A smile crosses my face, and I swim up to run my fingers over the collection of sea glass Ryan inlaid into the rock. He had to carve out a portion for every piece to bind it perfectly and must've spent so much time creating this place for me—for us.

"Do you like it? I think we're in a great location between the colony and the cove with access to an island, yet still a close enough swim to California within a day," he says, assessing my face for a reaction. "I mean, if you prefer me to build us another somewhere el—"

I throw myself through the water at him, kissing the thought right from his mind before he can even dare finish it. Ryan chuckles, releasing bubbles against my lips. He tugs me with him to the floor to gaze around. His taut chest puffs with pride, feeling all the good emotions coursing through me. I never expected him to create such a place of our own when we have so many places to live, and I appreciate his thoughtfulness.

He rolls on top of me, framing my face with his elbows, his caudal fin fanning over mine. "You always worry about everyone and everything else all the time, but even you need a break. I wanted to give you somewhere we could just get away."

"It's perfect," I think to him, running my finger across his bare chest. "Like you. I love it. It's the best present you could have given me apart from your love and life and your promise of forever."

He slides his tail against mine, shifting me in the sand. "Always and forever, Luna. Happy Winter Solstice."

I smile. "Happy Winter Solstice. I don't know how I'll

even top this."

Smirking, he says, "This is only the first part of your gift."

My mouth drops open. "Ryan, there's more?"

"You're not the only one who likes giving gifts. The next is a pod effort though. So, you can't give me all the credit. We thought you could use something special. It was going to wait until nightfall, but…"

"My rebel body," I finish for him. "Trying to ruin things."

"Hey, I love that beautiful body of yours, and nothing could ruin things for us. I mean it," he says, smiling.

"You're right," I say, trailing my hands to the back of his tail to press into him.

"So, do you want to swim back for the rest of your surprise or we could…enjoy our home for a while."

As much as my excitement wants me to drag Ryan away, I want nothing more than to remain here for a bit longer to appreciate what must've taken him weeks to do. All those times he said he was hunting probably ended with him here for a bit.

"I'm not sure I want to ever leave," I say into his mind, shifting up to kiss him. "My heart's not ready yet, and neither is the rest of me."

His eyes glimmer, drinking me in. "I was hoping you'd say that. Now hold that thought."

Ryan swims into another room of our underwater home and returns with a few woven kelp blankets. "A gift from Gi," he says. "For the blanket forts."

I laugh. "I love this...and you. Especially you."

"Welcome home, Luna."

"Home," I say.

Nothing has ever sounded better.

PERFECT WINTER SOLSTICE

MY BACK HITS THE soft sand next to Ryan, and he flips on top of me, shielding me from a cresting wave. I hold up my palm, freezing it in place so it blankets us in sparkling light. Calming the water, I let it caress our skin instead of colliding into us.

"Ah, come on." Giselle's voice echoes through the air. "I can't sneak up on you merpeople anywhere without getting a show, can I?"

Rosy blush crawls up Ryan's neck to bloom red splotches on his face. I laugh and flick my hand, sending a wave in Giselle's direction. She yelps and scrambles right into Sun's arms as he strolls in our direction from the community still a good distance away.

Ryan rolls off me and helps me to my feet, shuffling us back into waist-high water. I rinse off and kick my way back to the beach. Ryan stays right behind me, his human rationale returning in full force. No matter how often I talk to Giselle about there being nothing wrong with nudity, she clings onto her humanity as much as Ryan, and she can't help herself from teasing him. Even Ava's adapted to a mermaid life as she balances the land and sea with Carter. She's taken to following old customs while creating new ones that better help everyone adapt.

Giselle places her hands on her hips. "You brazen merpeople. I swear. Luna really converted you to the Naked Side, hasn't she?"

"You say that like it's a bad thing," I say. "I happen to love that my mate is brave enough to run me into the water while we're—"

"Okay, okay," she says. "I don't even want to know. It was bad enough that you kept...never mind. Everything is great. It's a beautiful morning. The sun's about to shine. The holidays are near. I'm with my soul sister and brother, my boyfriend."

"Don't forget your cousin," Talia says, kicking her way down the beach from the trees with Tide beside her. "Who comes bearing clothing."

Tide hands Talia a bag, and she skips the distance to me and Ryan. I dust off and change into my bikini before shrugging into the sundress. Ryan dresses behind me, wearing only swim trunks like every other merman who surfaces from the water to the cove.

"I saw you and Princess Luna rushing to the surf unprepared," Tide says to Ryan. "With the new guests around, I thought you might be uncomfortable returning to the community as is."

"Isn't he thoughtful?" Talia asks.

My smile widens as I glance between the two of them. "Tide has always been so amazing to all the colonies."

"And thank the ocean for that today," Giselle says. "The cove is a transitional colony not one for nudists, though I'm sometimes not sure anymore."

"Would it be so bad?" Sun muses. "Your body stirs such—"

Giselle covers his mouth with her hand, tipping her head back to laugh loud enough that I'm sure the whole island could hear her. "At least the pirates haven't converted."

I smirk. "Who says they haven't? My crew is pretty proud of their body art. They'll show anyone."

Ryan slides one arm across my chest to hug me from behind while holding out his other to bump fists with Tide. The gesture reminds me of how mermen bump tails in the ocean as a form of greeting or appreciation. "I'll mention your interest next time, Gi," Ryan teases, making Giselle fake glare at him. Turning to Tide, he adds, "And thanks for looking out, dude. This morning was...spur of the moment."

Tide grins without saying anything, and Sun pats Ryan on the back.

"Mermen," Talia says, turning to Giselle. "They really do go to great lengths to help each other out."

"I appreciate it," I say, smiling.

"So do I. Your ass was the last thing I expected to see when you told us to meet you guys here, Ryan." She swirls her finger at him. He must have caught someone swimming and relayed a message without me hearing. So sneaky, but I love how much effort Ryan's putting into my surprises. "Did you accidentally transform or something? That happened to me two weeks ago right in the middle of a visit with my mom. She makes me so nervous. I swear, she'll be the reason I have trouble remaining on land."

Ryan only shrugs without giving away the fact that it was me who accidentally transformed. "It happens. I haven't had much time to adjust with having to be on the surface all the time, but that's going to change."

I blink a few times at his words, his fake excuse to hide my inability to keep it together the last month digging into me deeper than it should.

Accidental transformations were one of the reasons human-born merpeople were taken to sea to adjust, but the laws have changed since Ava became queen. Now, we're cautious but not overly petrified over the situation. And Ryan hasn't even accidentally transformed once. He's been connected to the sea all his life. But me? I think surfacing broke the connection I have no matter how close I am to the sea with my ocean magic.

"What?" Giselle and Talia ask, turning to me at Ryan's revelation, one we haven't really cemented, especially after what Wren did. Or what my dad thinks about Ryan's healing ability. Not to mention my sometimes out of control magic. Unlike Ava, I didn't take to the sea to travel to all the colonies. I haven't been around much since my coupling ceremony to Ryan unless merpeople ventured to me.

"I—I don't know for sure. It was a thought. Not permanently. We just—"

"We'll tell you all more when things get set," Ryan says, finishing for me.

Giselle stares at me, tilting her head. A dozen emotions fly from her to me, but something confuses her. She opens and closes her mouth, giving me another once over. It takes Sun scooping her off her feet to sit on his shoulders to get her to break eye contact. And now I feel just as confused. Ryan's words set off a thought in her mind that reminds me of earlier when she realized Tide became unavailable because of Talia's interest. It's the same what's-happening-with-my-instincts look.

I open my mouth to ask Giselle what's on her mind, but a loud whistle sounds through the air, reminding me of the watchmen on the Ocean's King. Turning, I gaze at the aqua horizon for signs of boats, but it's as empty as usual.

Another whistle cuts through the air, and I turn to the others, realizing they're all smiling at me.

"I think that's the captain's call," Ryan says, nudging me forward.

Narrowing my eyes, I search his face for a hint he doesn't give. I must not be moving fast enough for everyone, because Talia takes my hand and pulls me with her. Ryan jogs ahead of us, turning around to walk backward to face me.

The morning light peeking from the horizon sets his skin aglow, reminding me of our first date and how we watched the sunrise from the *Sea Princess* when I took him to the glass beach near La Tortuga Point. That day, I had no idea this was where our adventure would lead, and I've never been happier no matter what battles we faced to get here. Because we were together, and I had my pod. And the sea. My perfect life couldn't get more perfect.

Until now.

"Happy early Winter Solstice, Luna!" Ava's sweet voice echoes over the hum of the ocean.

My eyes widen at the sight of her standing in the sand outside the cottages. Carter waves from a ladder where one of the fishermen holds it in place as Carter finishes securing lights that look like clear orbs of water summoned by ocean magic. Colorful lights twirl around the palm trees, and someone built the most amazing sand castle that looks just like Pearlestria along with hints of the human holidays such as snowmen with mermaid tails in the sand.

"What are you doing here? You should be preparing for the Winter Solstice," I say, closing the space to hug Ava.

Carter hops down from the ladder and hugs us both. "Someone told us a pirate stole your holiday cheer."

"So we came right away," Ava adds. "Pearlestria is all set. Starla is finishing the last minute stuff."

"But—"

Ava hugs me tighter. "This is your year to celebrate and let the rest of us handle the planning. I command you to stop worrying about everyone else. No more arguing, okay? I spoke with Attilonious, and he promised to behave and take over the rehabilitation of those lost at sea for us until after Christmas."

I frown. I can't help it. "I don't know, Ava. I want to, but something—"

She pulls away. "No, it's a command. Today we're going

to have some fun and then come tonight we're heading back to sea to enjoy the rest of our holiday."

Ryan turns me around to face him. "Listen to our queen, because I think this morning was a sign that you need a vacation."

"This is like a vacation."

"From the land," he says.

Ava glances between me and Ryan, her brows furrowing lower on her head. Giselle steps up beside her, and they whisper to each other, giving me the same look of confusion from earlier. Now, I'm really curious as to what's making them stare at me like I've grown two heads or something.

Touching my shoulder, Ava says, "Please, Luna. I know you want to take care of the world, but I want to take care of you. More than ever. I just—"

"So weird, Aves. I feel it too," Giselle whispers.

I grimace. "You two are freaking me out." I keep my voice low because they do out of habit. If Ava and Giselle think whispering in front of our mates is important, then I do it too. It's not often Giselle doesn't shout out what's on her mind.

Ava and Giselle share a curious look again, tilting their heads to each other and then Ava says, "Hey, Carter, why don't you guys all go hunt some breakfast for us?"

Okay, now I know something is up. I automatically turn

my attention to Talia and wonder if it has to do with her, and they just can't recognize it since they're still getting the hang of their mermaid intuition and instincts.

"I'd be happy to go alone, Queen Ava," Tide says, glancing at Talia.

Ava doesn't respond to him right away. Her eyes bore into me in a gaze I can feel sink deep beneath my skin. She's quiet long enough that I shift on my feet and hug my arms around myself. Tide clears his throat, finally breaking her attention on me. She blinks a few times, struggling to gather her thoughts, and it really starts to freak me out.

"No, it's cool, Tide," Carter says, speaking for her. "We can all go together. Right, Ryan and Sun?"

Ryan nods, coming closer to me. He can't see the weirdness both me and Carter can see in Ava. "You okay with that?"

I smile, suddenly starving at the thought more so than needing to know what's going through my best friends' minds. "There's nothing I want more than for you to feed me."

He chuckles. "You got it."

Ava and Giselle stand quietly as we watch the mermen joke and strip right on the beach, already in competition mode for their hunt. Talia slides up next to me and links our fingers together, staring after Tide.

"Someone tell me what's going on," she says, keeping her voice low. "You three are acting stranger than I'm used to."

I glance at Talia before turning to Ava and Giselle. "Not me. Them. They're still not used to knowing things about mermen without people having to say them."

Talia presses her lips together. "Oh."

"And he's definitely into you, Talia," Ava says. "Off the market, so to speak. But I don't think that's why I feel this way."

She flushes, her cheeks turning rosy. "Are you sure you didn't overhear Tide ask to court me last night?"

"So, he did ask you!" I clap my hands at the news. I can't help it.

She nods, smiling. "I like him a lot."

"I knew it! I'm so happy for you, Talia."

Giselle gets between us. "Relax, Luna. You're going to freak her out. My mermaid instincts are going off like crazy," Giselle says, laughing nervously. She looks at Talia. "It's definitely Luna doing it to my senses. I thought something was different last night, but both you and Sun distracted me."

Ava nods. "I don't know what it means."

I raise both my hands up. "Try to explain it, and I can probably decipher it. But I don't feel anything strange or different apart from Talia."

Inhaling and exhaling, Ava shifts her gaze from Talia to Giselle and finally stops back on me. "Why do I have this nagging urge to drag you into the sea and to take care of you?

It's intense and confusing me."

Talia squeezes my fingers, furrowing her brows. "I'm kind of jealous I don't get to feel what you feel."

"Don't worry, Lia," Giselle says, using the name Tide gave Talia. "You make my senses crazy too. I'm not sure how I'm going to ever get used to these weird super powers. Every time I see you with Tide, all I want to do is talk about courting and mermen dating."

"And don't forget about helping her plan her future coupling ceremony," I say, bouncing on my feet at the thought.

Sighing, Giselle nudges my shoulder with her hand. "Take it down a notch. You're going to scare her if you mention how excited you are about the seas flourishing."

"Oh, Ocean!" Ava screeches, her blue eyes widening. She waves her hands around, her revelation making her dance in her spot like she can't help it. "Oh, my God. That's it! That's why I feel like this."

Giselle's mouth drops open, and she searches me from head to toe. "Whoa, Aves. You're right."

Talia turns to stand next to them to give me a once over. "What are you two talking about?"

I inhale a sharp breath at the realization as they narrow their focus on my stomach, and everything about the last few weeks clicks into place and now makes perfect sense. My heart drifting to sea, my accidental transformations, Ryan's unintentional urge to build us a home of our own...

And Ava and Giselle confirm it. Mermaids know first. It's instinctual. It's how our pods and colonies work. We help and take care of each other through all of life's stages.

"I think I'm pregnant," I whisper, bringing my hands to my stomach.

"What?" Talia squeals. "How do you know? Are you sure? Should we go to civilization? What about a healer?"

"I—"

"Civilization?" Giselle asks. "I'm pretty sure mermaids don't surface for pregnancy tests."

Talia blushes and laughs. "I'm still learning about all this."

Giselle hugs her. "Me too. I guess I should've paid more attention to all of Starla's instinct lessons, because she insists I keep watch on Ava."

Ava steps closer. "You're not the only one who ignores Starla," she tells Giselle, her cheeks competing with Talia's over whose can burn the brighter shade of red. "And second, I don't know exactly how Luna knows, but I'm definitely sure. As queen, I see everyone's sparks, and..." She holds up her hand to my stomach without touching me. "I see a new one."

I peer down where her hand hovers, narrowing my gaze, noticing the faint blip of light beating in the same rhythm of my own heart. It's so small and barely noticeable that I'm not sure I'd have seen it without Ava, but the tiny spark brings me so much joy I'm suddenly breathless. I wish I had paid more attention to myself, but I'm always busy looking at Ryan.

"How could I miss this?" I feel like I should've known, but the mother figures in my pod are farther than I like. Nalani, Ryan's mom, visits from Reefaria but it's been weeks. And Starla is in San Francisco.

"Oh, you know. Scrooge father-in-law keeping you busy. Unruly pirates. Party planning. Ocean harming fishermen, your hot mate that you can never take your eyes off. Your investment in Talia's—and everyone else's love lives, not to mention me and our land family," Giselle says, tapping her index finger to her palm, counting out her reasons. "But who cares! Luna, you're going to make the sea flourish...and all I want to do is feed you."

Ava laughs. "And take her back to sea."

Talia touches her fingers over my hand on my stomach for a second before throwing her arms around me. Ava and Giselle follow suit, enveloping me in a wave of excitement and love that quickly washes away my surprise.

I knew a life such as this was what I always wanted, but I was afraid all the work aboard the Ocean's King, the worry I carry about the surface and land and sea, would hold me and Ryan back from such an occasion. I projected my desire to see the ocean flourish onto others, but really, the yearning has been inside me all along.

"This is amazing, Luna," Ava says. "And I want everything to be perfect for you. You have to tell me about the traditions."

"Mermaids throw a celebration, of course," I say. "After I tell Ryan."

"When?" Giselle asks.

I shrug. "Tonight, I guess. That way I can show him. He doesn't know everything this kind of thing entails and might not notice yet otherwise, and it's best in the sea with the moon. A mermaid's biggest struggle is the surprise because mermen have instincts too."

Ava grins. "Tonight it is. It'll be the perfect way to start off Winter Solstice."

Tonight I'll once again change Ryan's life forever.

Giselle claps her hands. "I can't wait!"

MAKE THE SEAS FLOURISH

"WE HAVE AT LEAST another hour," Ava says, refilling my glass of pineapple juice. "You know they won't come back until someone catches something the size of one of us."

I finish eating the last sugar cookie from the pile Ava decorated like Christmas trees and snowmen. "Yeah, especially without our help," I say with a laugh. I love how much Ryan's embraced his nature, but he would've spent all night hunting something for my dad if I didn't insist he let me lure a fish in.

Giselle plops the rest of her pancakes onto my plate. She adds extra syrup like I love and dollops a blob of whipped cream on top. "Good thing we're strong, independent women or else we'd starve."

"Good thing," I say, poking at the pancake, my stomach so full I'm pretty sure I'll explode if I eat another bite. "Though I'm not sure my stomach can survive all your independence, Gi."

Talia laughs. "You do look like you're going to sink instead of swim when we hit the water."

Ava smirks at Giselle. "Then we will swim her."

I laugh again and then groan, clutching my stomach. "I love you all, but Ryan's going to think something is wrong if I don't devour their catch. I could probably go without eating for another month."

Giselle plunks her elbows on the table and sighs. "Am I going to feel like this the whole time? It's still so freaking weird. I don't even have the urge to feed Sun like this."

"It's our bond," I say. "All pods have the need to take care of their family. I think that's why you both came to shore to be with me. It's instinctual even if we didn't know."

"When do you think...?" Ava asks. "I mean, I guess it's none of my business. I was just wondering because Starla told me that it's in our control as mermaids if we allow our mates to—" She pauses, licking her lips. "You know, and you also know her. She's dying for me and Carter to..."

"Make the seas flourish," Giselle finishes with a laugh. "I remember the looks on our moms' faces when she said that right in front of everyone at Thanksgiving, trying to get your mom on board."

"Us future grandmers must stick together," Ava says, doing her best Starla impression.

"She sounds persistent," Talia says.

I smile. "She's just excited about the next generation. So am I, to be honest. Ryan and I have talked about this since we coupled. And now that I think about it, it was probably that night at Thanksgiving. We were imagining our futures and talking about taking some time to explore the sea more."

"Remind me to keep all thoughts like that off my mind," Giselle says. "My mom struggles already. If it just takes a little extra desire and sex...crap. Expanding pods sounds contagious, because merbabes are so cute and cuddly when they let you hold them and—"

Ava giggles and smacks Giselle's arm with the back of her hand. "Stop it. It takes more than that."

"Ugh. Luna loves everything about this," Giselle says, taking her plate of pancakes back to shove one in her mouth. "I bet she's hoping we all make the sea flourish together."

I grin. I can't help it. Of course I do, though I know neither of them are ready. They're human born. They love the land where it's expensive. Me and Ryan? As much as we love the land, our place is at sea. "Just imagine. If only it didn't make us accidentally transform or head to sea until our merbabes are old enough to transform. I know you're still gaining control."

Giselle gasps. "Oh, my God! It was *you* today!"

I bare my teeth at her. "At the worst moment ever."

"This is why expecting mermaids return to sea immediately, right?" Ava asks. "Besides the time after."

Talia taps her fork on her plate, remaining quiet as she listens to the three of us talk about things she won't have to worry about until she and Tide decide to couple. Her bottom lip pouts the longer she stares, and it takes me tapping her with my foot under the table to get her to look at me.

"At least they used to," I say. "I don't have to worry about revealing our secret, and we have this cove."

My words bring a smile to Talia's face. She reaches over and squeezes my hand, and both Giselle and Ava hug me again. I never knew I'd have such support in my life growing up. After my mom gave herself back to the sea, it was always me and Dad. And then he lost his ocean magic, and it was just me. But now? My life is so full of love and hope and a future complete with people on land and in the sea who'll assure life will be the best.

A knock sounds on the door to the cabin, and Ava motions for me to stay sitting while she answers it. I lean back in my chair to get a better view of our visitor and spot the scruffy captain from the fishing vessel at my door through the crack in the curtain of the window.

"Is the princess here?" he asks Ava, keeping his eyes trained on her instead of trying to look inside the cabin where I sit just out of his view. "Sandra mentioned we'd be relocating to another part of the island, and my men and I don't want to."

Ava runs her fingers through her hair. Shifting, she peeks at me behind her, and I shrug. "I'm sorry. That's where your new guide lives, so staying here isn't an option. Attilonious will be here any minute to retrieve you."

"Attilonious?" the captain questions. "Who the hell is that?"

"Me." My dad's booming voice sounds through the air louder than the waves. I can't see him from this position, but I can sense him approaching in his authoritative manner, probably all scowling and rigid, surely intimidating as he stretches his full height out. It's how he approaches all strangers.

The captain startles, his eyes widening at the sheer command of the single word Dad utters. I quickly get to my feet and scramble to the door to push past Ava. Dad said he'd watch the fishermen for Winter Solstice, but he never did agree to be nice to them. And Dad's a lot like Wren, using fear for compliance.

"And staying here is not an option. I see you already believe you're on some vacation, when this is a transitional island not made to bring you joy until you've earned the right. You will also respect my daughter's decision without complaint and be gracious you have the chance to help her build a great future for the seas despite the damage you cause."

The captain balls his hands into fists. "The chance? Not like it was a damn choice. I had a great—"

Dad lifts the captain off his feet before he can even finish the sentence, shaking him two stern times off the ground. "You were the problem!"

Oh, Ocean. I was worried about this. Dad might have good intentions, but his emotions always ran hot when it came to how he thought the sea needed protecting, and sinking ships was his solution. It's how he suggested I handle the pirate problem before I got it under control. While these fishermen don't threaten the union of land and sea, they still stand in our way to bettering our world, something I'm more determined about now that I'll forever have the best pieces of me and Ryan living apart from us within our merbabe.

The captain swings his arm out and punches Dad in the face, but Dad doesn't even react to the man's force. He remains sturdy in his spot like the trees along the beach. The man winces and yells out, "Put me down, asshole!"

"You need to understand who's in charge here," Dad says, shaking him again.

I rush toward my dad and the captain, but Ava grabs my

hand, pulling me back. Dad throws the captain right into the waves. A few more voices sound from the community, and I realize that the rest of the fishermen stand in trepidation. With the way fear mars all their faces, I doubt I'm going to convince any of them to follow my dad now.

"Princess Luna." The old man—Gus—wrings his hands together. "We were under the assumption that you would be helping us. You can't send us with that guy."

"My daughter has more important things to do," Dad says, stepping closer to the old man. "And this is my gift to her." Which isn't exactly the gift I had imagined he'd give me when he made the offer. How can I leave these men now? What if Dad does more damage? I depend on them wanting to join my crew by their own free will and not because they were forced. It'll be too risky. I can't have them turning against my loyal crew. It's dangerous.

"Princess—"

Dad crosses the space faster than Gus can even utter a word and lifts the old man off his feet too. Gus hollers and flails, not trying to fight my dad but trying his best to get out of the strong hold my dad locks him in. Ava summons a wave tall enough to reach the tops of the palm trees. Dad hesitates, reconsidering following through with his plan to throw Gus. Glaring and grumbling at Ava and her gigantic wave, he finally sets Gus back on his feet before moving a dozen feet away with enough space to get the scared crew to relax a teensy bit.

"Attilonious," Ava says, her soft voice dripping with annoyance I can almost feel in the air. "You're supposed to welcome the members of Luna's new crew and not try to control them with fear. It's not our way. We want people to join our efforts willingly and not be a risk to everyone." She says exactly what's on my mind. Ava and I have always seen things in sync, and I've never been more grateful to have the honor to be part of her pod even without blood bonds. Our bond lies in the ocean magic we share.

Dad crosses his arms over his broad chest, straightening his back more to attempt to intimidate Ava, though she's as unfazed by his height like I am. If anything, she appreciates that his tall frame blocks the sun from her eyes. "You don't understand—"

I throw my hands up before Dad can start arguing with Ava, forcing her to unleash a wave on him to get him to cool off. His heated anger escalates rather quickly no matter how much he tries to control it. "You know what? This doesn't seem like it's going to work. The men obviously don't want to learn from my dad—who I don't think is quite the right fit to teach them the new ways of the seas—and I should get to know them better anyway. Ryan and I will just stay here and help them. If I have to miss the holiday, then I miss it. There's always next year. At least I can guarantee Ryan that we'll be in

Pearlestria for sure."

"No, Luna. This isn't just any holiday. It's Winter Solstice," Giselle says, coming up behind me. She places her hands on my shoulders and leans into me. "And what about the—"

Talia covers Giselle's mouth before she can say anything about the surprise we were planning for Ryan. "I'll do it. I'll stay here. I know the workings of our crew, and I technically don't celebrate Winter Solstice."

"And that's why you shouldn't stay here. You should be with our crew. They were going to gather to watch the big swim. I bet Tide was going to ask you to join him on the surface for the event."

She frowns, glancing from me to the fishermen. "He did ask me, but it's not a big deal. Seriously, Luna."

I pout my bottom lip. "I can't ask you to do this for me. It's a big deal for the both of you as newly courting mates."

She turns me to face her. "And it's a big deal for you and Ryan as newly coupled mates. So, how about we compromise? We can take them with us. You said the crew was going to gather anyway. I don't see why they have to stay here." She turns to the fishermen. "You all will behave, right?"

"They could fight and try to steal the ship they're on. That could end badly," I say, kicking my bare foot into the sand. "I don't trust them." Not to mention that if they did try to fight, my crew might throw them overboard, and I don't want to fish fishermen from the water. I'll be too nervous to even enjoy the big swim.

Ava comes up to me and places a hand on each of my shoulders. "Then trust the ocean. Trust our magic. Trust us."

A million what-ifs cross my mind. The cove assures that people who learn our secret can't run off and escape to tell the world. It's the place I build trust with the people who also have to trust me in return. And I couldn't possibly leave them here alone or with my dad. This is our cove, not theirs. I'm afraid if I leave them they'll have too much time to think about how to escape or that the time will make it too hard to get them to adapt to my crew. Acting quickly and now will help, especially because I don't have a lot of time.

"I don't know," I say, blowing strands of loose hair from my face. "You remember what happened last time."

She wets her lips, sorrow darkening her sky blue eyes. Of course she remembers the last time I brought people to the island after revealing our secret. I don't think anyone will ever forget Wren's introduction to the mermaid life or his treacherous chief mate, Titus, who nearly cost me my future with Ryan.

"Luna!" Like the sea summons him by my heart's request, Ryan's familiar voice shouts through the air, drawing my attention from Ava and the others and to the sea.

Except instead filling my heart with love and relief, his emerging from the ocean sinks my heart into my stomach. He and the other three mermen follow behind him empty-handed, kicking their way to shore. They would have never returned without finishing a hunt without a reason, and Ryan's emotions bat at me in a rush of annoyance.

"Ah hell," Giselle whispers, surely feeling the emotions that have stolen her mate's smile from his face as well. "What now?"

Ava, Giselle, and Talia realize what I do about our mates and being empty-handed and rush to catch up to me as I break out into a sprint to meet Ryan in the waves. He scoops me up to kiss me, greeting me with all his love instead of automatically telling us what's going on. He always greets and leaves me with affection, making a point to try to assure my happiness even if we both know something bothers him.

"Enough kissing," I whisper into his lips, sliding my hands over his muscular shoulders. "What's wrong?"

"Just one more," Ryan says, brushing his lips to mine for another sweet moment. He rests his forehead to mine to block out my view of the world, begging me to focus my attention solely on him. "I've been feeling your anxiety and annoyance for a few minutes, and I don't want to add to whatever has stolen the bliss and excitement my surprises brought to you this morning."

"Ryan." I stick my bottom lip far enough out that it grazes his, tempting him to suck it between his teeth.

"Plus, you taste like syrup, and I'm starving," he says, resisting my plea of his name.

I laugh against his mouth, giving in to him. How could I not? All he wants is to make me happy, and that's all I've ever wanted for him.

"See? Much better." He pulls away so that I can focus on his handsome face and vibrant sea glass green eyes I can lose myself in. Turning to the beach, he spots my dad sitting in the sand and the fishermen glaring at all of us from their spot in the shade of the tall palm trees. "But I can see why you're stressing. I'm going to assume the introduction between your dad and the fishermen didn't go well, right?"

I suck in my top lip between my teeth, whipping my head back and forth hard enough to send my black tresses pelting Ryan's face. "You can say that. Dad threw the captain into the waves and nearly tried to with Gus. I was thinking it might not be such a good idea to lea—"

Ryan interrupts me with a kiss and releases a groan. "Luna, we might not have a choice and not because of Winter Solstice. Sandy found us while we were hunting and—"

"Oh, no. Has something happened with the crew?" I ask without letting him finish.

"Try not to stress too much," he says without giving me

much more. And I'm not sure he will at this point.

A dozen thoughts hit me at once as I think about all the horrible possibilities that could go wrong. I feel like I can't leave anyone alone. I might as well call my fleet to the island, but then that leaves the seas unprotected. "Is it Wren? What did he do?"

He shifts his eyes away from mine, giving away a clue that it is about his dad. "I don't know how bad any of this is. No one is hurt or anything. We might even be able to wait until after Winter Solstice." Squeezing his eyes closed, he pulls me close again to rest his forehead to mine. "Actually, I think that's exactly what we should do."

"Ryan, tell me what's really going on. You can't make these sorts of decisions without me, and you most definitely can't just kiss me and hope for Winter Solstice miracles." I cup his face and glare at him to show I'm serious. I know he's trying to save my holiday cheer, but I fear it might be beyond salvageable.

He has the nerve to chuckle and kiss me a dozen more times, using my love of him to get me to relax in the process. Sneaky. "You bet I can."

I purse my lips, trying so hard not to return the smile he gives me. "Ryan."

He snuggles against me. "Okay, okay. I'll tell you, but only because I don't want to risk you turning your annoyance on me." He turns to look at someone behind me, possibly Giselle or Ava, and whatever they do gets him to take a breath. "My dad is definitely getting demoted from chief mate. I'm going to bring him here myself for stealing your holiday cheer."

"What?" Panic stirs inside me, battling with the good emotions Ryan summons from me. It must be something awful if Ryan thinks we should bring his dad here and away from the crew. He's one of our best. "Oh, Ocean. What did he do?"

By the grimace crossing his face, Ryan doesn't want to tell me more. "You have to promise to stay calm."

"I will."

"I mean it, Luna. This isn't the end of the world, and like I said, it probably can wait until after the holidays."

"Don't tell her, Ryan," Giselle says from somewhere behind me. Sun must've already told her.

"I command you to carry your mate to sea and head to Pearlestria," Ava adds.

I thrust myself back in Ryan's arms, nearly causing him to drop me. Dangling upside down, I glare at my two best friends and cousin as they stand with their mates. I can't believe Ava went there with her use of authority, but I know why she did it. She's being protective.

Ryan pulls me back up and glances at Ava. "I have to tell her or she's not going to stop thinking about it." If he knew about the surprise I have for him, he'd definitely agree with Ava instead of giving into my need to know. He draws his attention back to me. "My dad's gone rogue. He stole the Ocean's King and left Darren in the tender boat."

"What?" I screech. "Damn it, Wren!" Covering my mouth in surprise, I stand in shock at my sudden reaction. While I'm disappointed, I can't say I'm too shocked, especially after the stunt he pulled with the fishermen. I take a breath, calming my racing heart. "You know what? You're right. He can wait until after Winter Solstice. The ocean won't let him get far. He's testing his boundaries like my dad did when he tried to swim from the cove."

Ryan engulfs me in another hug, combing his fingers through my hair. "I'm glad you agree. But I should tell you that it's more than him stealing the Ocean's King."

I groan. "Please don't tell me—"

He nods. "He's going after another fishing vessel. It's why he forced Darren to abandon ship because he knew he would stop him."

Shifting on my feet, I turn to look at Ava having a quiet discussion with Carter as the others remain silent to see what we plan to do. As much as I can see Ava wanting to stick to her command and have Ryan take me to Pearlestria, she won't actually follow through with it. We're in this together.

She catches me staring at her and offers me a small smile,

her gaze trailing from my eyes to glance at my stomach. She zones in on my belly so intensely that I wonder if Ryan or the other mermen will notice her strange behavior. It's then that I realize she's not the only one acting differently. I've let go of Ryan to cradle myself, something I don't do naturally. A dozen emotions cross Ava's face and she turns to Giselle, who nods at her.

"Luna," Ava says, grabbing her mate's hand. "Carter and I will handle Wren. Giselle, Sun, Talia, and Tide will see to it that the fishermen here are taken care of and brought safely to our waters over Pearlestria, where they can keep a good eye on them." Turning to Ryan, she says, "And I want you to do as I already said and take Luna—"

Cramps suddenly seize my muscles, setting off my mermaid transformation without my permission. It happens so quickly that no one has the chance to react before I hit the sand and a wave rushes over my head to drag me into the bay, summoned by my magic reacting to me. It's like the ocean knew I was going to argue with Ava and decided not to give me a choice in the matter.

I flick my tail, though I don't get far. Three pairs of hands latch onto me and pull me to the surface. I spit and clear my lungs of the ocean water to see Ryan, Giselle, and Ava all holding onto a part of me. They all look at each other, and Giselle and Ava both start laughing, their faces reddening in the warm light of the sun. I'll have no choice but to just tell Ryan my surprise for him if they keep acting this way. I thought mermaids struggled with surprising their mates because of mermen instincts, but now I'm pretty sure they only have those instincts because of overly doting mermaids.

"I think I have her," Ryan says, tilting his head to give both Ava and Giselle a funny look.

They glance at each other, their cheeks now flaming red, and the two of them start laughing even harder, almost hysterically, making Ryan frown even more.

"Of course you do," Giselle says, smiling. She pokes his shoulder with her finger and steps away, clutching Ava's hand to get her to let me go.

"Why don't you transform back, and we can work out a plan before Ryan takes you to Pearlestria. You can be there to run the ceremony in case Carter and I are late." Ava touches her hand to the bend of my tail, begging me with her eyes to do as she asks. "Sound good?"

I frown. This isn't fair to Ava or the rest of my pod. Plus, the idea of running the whole ceremony scares me. I'd prefer to handle Wren. "I can't."

"I didn't think I was ready last year either—"

I hold up my hand to cut her off, not wanting her to know she's right. "Ava, I have to take care of Wren. This is my duty. You shouldn't have to. It's better if we handle it. Ryan knows his dad best."

"But—"

Ryan hugs me like squeezing me just right will get me to agree to Ava's plan. "Come on. We'll discuss this on shore."

"Fine, but you should know my spark is set." Shutting my eyes, I will for my transformation to take hold, but nothing happens. No cramps. No tightening muscles. Nothing. I can't do it. The sea refuses to let me go.

"Luna?" Ryan asks, touching my chin. "You okay?"

"No," I blurt, tears burning my eyes. "I can't change back. Everything is just so out of control and—" I nearly tell him I'm pregnant right this second, but something stops me. It doesn't feel right. My instincts say to wait until everything is situated so Ryan can enjoy the news. "I need us to take care of your dad. We know him better than anyone."

"Luna," Ava and Giselle say in unison. "Please reconsider. Let us help you," Ava adds.

"How about I check in on him, and if I have to, I'll call the royal guard to drag the Ocean's King to Pearlestria? That way, we'll still make it back for the celebration. You know it's better this way. Wren listens to me," I say, forcing myself to smile.

Giselle opens her mouth to argue. "What about—"

I shake my head, knowing exactly what she wants to know without letting her attempt to hint about me telling

Ryan the news. "It'll just have to wait."

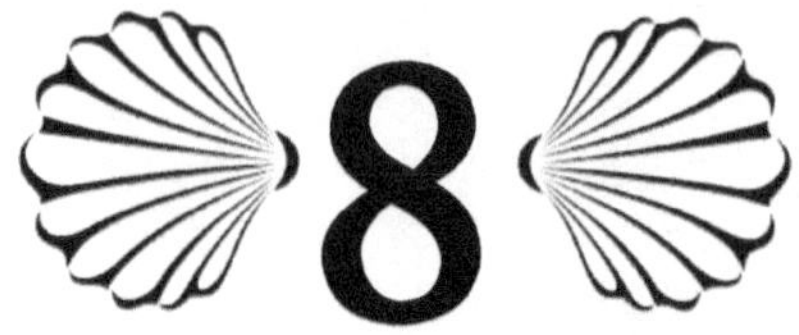

MAGICAL TIME

I BREAK THROUGH THE surface and spit out water. Darren waves at me from the stern of the Hurricane, anchored not far from where we left the Ocean's King by Ryan's favorite uninhabited island before we took the fishermen to the cove.

The salty sea air engulfs me, and I inhale a few deep breaths, hoping that it'll help ease the stress squeezing my chest.

Ryan transforms under me, sliding his hands up my tail from behind until he reaches my shoulders to break through. I shiver under his touch, his breath warm against my ear as he gasps for a moment from the strenuous swim. He practically flew through the water, not letting me help at all, and I know it's because he's determined to get everything taken care of in time to get to Pearlestria by sundown on Winter Solstice when the celebration starts.

Sliding into his swim trunks, he dresses and then nudges me to turn around. He trails his gaze from my lips and downward, appreciating me in my mermaid form like he always does. There's never a second I don't feel like the most beautiful mermaid he's ever seen. "Try to transform again."

I huff a breath and sink under, closing my eyes. I stay submerged for at least ten minutes with Ryan treading on the surface, watching me from above, his strong body begging me to follow his lead to return to my human form.

I quit after another minute and pop back up to Ryan. "I'm broken."

He smirks and kisses me, running his fingers through my drenched hair to push it behind my ears. "You're perfect. Probably just overly stressed. Come on. Let me help you up on the platform. You don't need legs with me. I'll gladly carry you anywhere."

His words prod at my heart, and a smile breaks through the pout I'm sure he's worried will never leave my face. Caressing his lips to mine once more, Ryan swims to the boat to hoist himself from the sea. Water runs in rivulets down his muscular, tan body, and I watch him shake off, admiring how his skin glistens in the sun.

He grins at me, allowing me to check him out before he holds his hand out and tugs me up, his muscles bulging with the action. He'd have never been able to lift me from the sea with one hand before, and I can't help but admire his new strength as a merman.

"I love that you're enjoying me right now," he whispers, setting me carefully on the platform.

I don't get the chance to respond that I'm most definitely enjoying every second with him despite the reason for surfacing because Darren rushes over.

"Are you okay, Luna?" Darren asks, squatting down to give me a hug and a kiss on the cheek. His voice remains light as usual, not giving away anything negative. He's always so kind and sweet to me, knowing how to talk to me. I can't help thinking about what it would have been like to have been raised by him and my mom together.

I lift and drop my shoulders, trying just as hard to keep my voice even. I know how much both he and Ryan hate to see me cry. "I should be asking you that. What Wren did—"

He chuckles, surprising me. "Was not exactly unexpected, but it's okay. I'm fine. It was actually pretty funny."

The sea and ocean magic surrounding a mermaid's favorite holiday must be getting to his head. Nothing about this situation is funny. Wren stole the Ocean's King and my crew. "Funny?" I ask, tilting my head to the side. I try to think of anything to make this funny but can't think of anything.

"He threatened a new crew of fishermen that he'd throw them to the mermaids. Not exactly as effective as his shark bit, but he threw me overboard and Sandy pulling me under might have scared them a bit. He hasn't hurt anyone at least."

"Yet." Wren might have changed from being a brutal pirate to innocent people, but now he directs his ruthlessness toward people he thinks deserve it.

"I don't think he will. Something just has him all wound up. He was upset after discovering the..." He lets his thought trail off. "I think you've turned him soft-hearted toward everything in the sea."

My annoyance melts away at the possibility of Wren being anything other than tough. "You think so?"

"I'm pretty sure he'd cuddle a shark if it'd allow him," Ryan says, sliding his hand under my tail to pull it across his lap.

I give him a pointed look, lowering my chin. "I'm about to arrange it."

Ryan wags his eyebrows at me, the thought of his dad attempting to cuddle anything that isn't a pile of treasure quite silly the longer I think about it. "I'll help you. Maybe then you'll find the will to transform again."

"So, there is a reason you're not climbing aboard," Darren says, shifting our conversation from Wren and to me.

I shrug. "It's stress. I really want to take Ryan to Pearlestria and all of this is making it hard on me." I nearly tell them both about what could possibly be the real reason I'm not transforming or how I worry I might not be able to until... Oh, Ocean. I need to ask a healer. I hate the thought of being bound to the sea for so long when Darren, Talia, and my dad reside on land. Not to mention my crew.

And now I'm freaking out by how unprepared I am.

I've always dreamed of the day I'd couple and expand my pod, but with the change in traditions and my reign as pirate queen, I haven't put more thought into making it work. I've been surviving on love and my instincts, just experiencing everything as it comes in my current.

Darren plops down to sit next to me on my other side at my admission. Wrapping his arm around my back, he hugs me without being prompted, just knowing that I need one. "We're going to fix this. Winter Solstice was always your mom's favorite holiday as well," Darren says. "And don't worry. Wren isn't too far away."

Ryan rests his hand on my tail. "We'll get him and drag him to the celebration whether or not he agrees."

A wave of water splashes over my tail, and Nalani hoists herself onto the ladder, surprising me. "Oh, no. You two are here. I'm sorry you've come all this way." She turns her attention to Ryan. "My son, I thought you'd call the guard. You two should be heading to Pearlestria. Everyone's been waiting for you with such great anticipation."

"This is our problem, Nalani," I say, speaking up. "Not the royal guard's."

Ryan scoops water from the sea to drizzle over my tail. "You know my mate. She worries about everyone else over herself."

Nalani drips water behind me, and I lean back to peer up at her haloed in light. She stares at me long and hard, giving me an intense look that sends my heart racing. It's the same weirdness Giselle and Ava gave me.

I try my best to ignore it and say, "I'm working on changing that. I want to take Ryan and head to sea for at least a little while. Ryan surprised me with a new home, so we can have a place close to everywhere we need to be."

Ryan smiles. "I felt it was a good time. Everything is under control, and—"

"Sort of under control," I murmur.

Darren nudges me. "It is. I'm telling you, Luna. Wren will come to his senses."

Nalani shifts behind me, the weight of her gaze still boring into me. "Now it all makes sense," she says without taking her eyes off mine. I knew she felt the same thing as Ava and

Giselle, and as a healer, she'd recognize her instincts.

"What do you mean?" Ryan asks, peering between us.

Nalani presses her lips together, staring at me with her intense green eyes. Without responding to Ryan, she strolls to the edge of the platform and dives right back into the sea, confusing all of us. She transforms into a mermaid and shoots up in front of me, hooking her hands around my tail to pull me back into the water. And the second our eyes meet, her whole face lights up, and she smiles. I don't have to say anything for her to confirm that she knows I'm expecting. She's not only considered a mother to me, but she's the best healer in Reefaria.

"My daughter," she says into my mind. With Ryan in his human form with Darren, he can't hear us. But I don't think Nalani would allow him to anyway. "My heart expands with such joy. Have you told Ryan?"

I smile and shake my head. "I just found out when Giselle and Ava surprised me at the cove."

"This is why you were planning to return to the sea," she murmurs, sinking lower to press her cheek to my stomach.

Laughing, I cradle her head against me. "Actually no, but it just happened to work out this way."

She pulls away, her smile dazzling the longer the news sinks in. "Even if you didn't plan it as so, your spark knows. Never underestimate or ignore your instincts. It's more important than ever."

"I couldn't ignore them even if I wanted to. I can't transform back," I say, pouting. The thought still gets to me, especially after how sad Talia was when Ava questioned it this morning. "I know it's tradition to return to sea, but I didn't realize I'd actually have to. And now with Wren? This isn't good."

Opening her arms, Nalani engulfs me into a hug. "It's better than good. It's amazing. And you should be able to transform, my daughter. The only thing that could hold you back is you. For those who emerge and live lives on land, the ability doesn't vanish. We only return to sea for our young until they can manage to transform not because we can't."

I inhale a huge breath of water. "That's what I thought. I just—oh, thank the ocean."

She giggles, releasing bubbles to float to the surface. "I'm sorry I haven't prepared you more, Luna. I knew the day would come, but I wasn't sure how soon seeing that Ryan was raised on the land."

"He's adapting faster to the sea than I have to the land," I say. "He might be human-born, but he does have the sea in his blood."

"And Wren sees that," she says. "He has instincts of his own. That man hasn't gotten to where he is on luck alone."

I groan. "That's what this is all about." I know it.

Wren isn't acting out because he's returning to his old ways. He must feel us drifting. Things haven't been so clear as to why the old pirate king would suddenly revert to his old ways until now. He must have heard Ryan and me discussing our future. It was never a secret that we'd take some time away from the surface, and that's always been Wren's hang up. He's always been afraid of losing his son.

Nalani pulls back and smoothes my floating hair. "I think you're right. But Wren will change his mind."

"If we can reach him."

"We will. My mate is tracking the Ocean's King. I'll take us to him. Then we can all head to Pearlestria together," Nalani says, reaching out to graze her fingers over my stomach. "What a magical time, don't you think? The colonies will be so thrilled to welcome you and Ryan home."

I nod. I can barely believe it. Home to Pearlestria. Home to the sea. And I can finally take Ryan with me. Him, me, and our future merbabe. Merry Winter Solstice to me.

HOLIDAY OF THIEVES

"WHAT ARE YOU THINKING?" Ryan asks. "I don't know what my mom said to you, but I love the way it makes you feel right now."

I grin, nuzzling my nose against his chest as he swims with me in his arms as we follow Nalani through the sea. The silhouette of the Hurricane blocks out the glittering sun above us, and I reach my hand over Ryan's shoulder to practice freezing the bubbles in its wake.

"I'm just dreaming about our future," I say. "Nalani and Sandy plan to move to Pearlestria to be closer to us. She can help you with your gift."

He glances down at me. "That's still so weird to me."

"Once you hone your skills, you'll help so many," I say. "My healer mate."

Running his hands up and down my back, he massages my tense muscles, making me moan against his skin. "I guess all those years helping my grandma must've sparked my skills."

"It helps that the ocean is free. The elders think that amazing things will evolve in the colonies now."

"I'm sure of it too. I can feel it."

Ryan dives deeper in the sea, navigating around a happily swimming pod of dolphins. They bolt around us, teasing Ryan in an attempt to get him to let go of me. He only holds me tighter, not giving into their desire to play. It's not the first time an overly friendly pod tried to play keep away with a mermaid against her mate.

"Oh, no." Nalani's voice trickles into my mind, igniting a blip of fear to battle it out with Ryan's light-hearted mood as he races to out swim the pod. In doing so, we come up to Nalani so quickly that she gets caught in Ryan's current, and it takes Ryan hooking his hand around her arm to get us all to come to a stop.

Easing away from Ryan's chest and wildly beating heart, I turn to Nalani peering around the open sea. The dolphins swim ahead, chattering away, and some of them breach out of the water to dive back under, creating all sorts of bubbles.

"What's wrong?" I ask Nalani, shooing away a curious male dolphin vying for both mine and Nalani's attention.

"I just got word from Sandy. It seems Wren threw a man overboard," she says.

I groan. "Did Sandy get him?"

She nods. "It was Ali. He's taken him to an island not far from here, but he had to abandon him to continue to follow Wren."

It's Ryan's turn to groan. Releasing my hand, he swims circles a few times around us, creating a whirlpool while keeping any interested dolphins away. They finally give up and continue on their way after a minute.

"You really think he's doing this as a way to try to get us to stay aboard the Ocean's King?" Ryan asks his mom. "Because all it's going to do is get him land bound."

Nalani darts her gaze to mine, hiding what seems to be a never-ending smile with her hand. "I think so."

"At least it wasn't one of the new hostages. I bet Ali stood up to him and that's how he got himself thrown overboard," Ryan says. "My dad knew someone wouldn't be far to help him."

I swim to Ryan to snuggle back in his arms, suddenly not wanting to be out of them. All I want to do is ask him to swim me to the house he built us and snuggle me despite the task at hand. It's so strange.

"I'll go tell Darren," Nalani says.

Ryan kisses me on the forehead and pulls away again. "Go with my mom. I think I know where the island is. If I'm right, it's a couple of minutes swim."

I don't let Ryan get far, my need to return to his arms far exceeding the normal amount of cuddles I want from him. Waving my hand, I cut him off with a cool current, knocking him off course. He spins to look at me in the water, and I swim forward and back into his arms.

He chuckles and glances up to Nalani, peering down at us from the surface. "Or you can tell Darren that Luna and I will be back in a few minutes."

She smiles and nods. "I'll catch up and help with Ali."

Ryan tightens his hold on me and darts off, practically flying through the water. My body aligns with his so no water gets between us, our stomachs touching and his heartbeat thrumming in my ear in sync with mine. A wave of calm washes over me, just relishing our closeness.

"I love you," I say to Ryan.

He tilts his chin to brush his lips to the top of my head. "I love you, too."

"Thanks for always being so amazing."

He chuckles. "As much as I love everything about your

sudden affection, I have to ask. What's up? Something feels different. A good different. So much so that I want to beg you to swim away with me and let the rest of the world handle my dad."

"I might let you," I say.

Adjusting me in his arms, he raises me higher so we're face-to-face instead of letting me continue to snuggle against his taut chest. Our hearts thud against each others, and Ryan uses one hand to pull the strands of hair veiling my face away.

I kiss him before he can even allow me to hear his thoughts. Something amazing bursts from me in a hot wave that has me pressing harder into Ryan, setting off his lust to crash over me. Deepening our kiss, Ryan slides his tongue into my mouth, running his hand down my back to clutch the backside of my tail to pull me even closer to him. Heat blossoms between us, sending tingles through my entire body, setting my spark aglow so brightly that it outshines the sunbeams trickling in from the surface.

"Luna, we should stop," he whispers. "I don't think I can stop myself from swimming us away if you don't."

I kiss him harder, practically devouring his lips, everything good between us throwing out the bad so I can forget it exists. "I don't want to. Take me to our home."

Ryan dives a few feet deeper. "But Ali."

"Will be fine."

Ryan slows down, easing back to look into my eyes. "Luna."

I only let him look at me for a second before I close the space between us again, a hunger to be with Ryan gripping my body so tightly that there is no way that I can ignore it. And Ryan's on the cusp of relenting to my needs.

"Luna," he whispers into my mind. "Are you sure? Because there's no way I'm going to deny you. This is what I wanted to do."

I hug him closer. "I'm sure."

"Okay then—"

One second we're flying through the water and in the next the shallows sneak up on us so quickly that Ryan can't slow down fast enough. He hits his back to the sand, the force stopping him but also making him let go of me, and I tumble head over tail through the waves until I land on the beach.

I spit out water, my chest heaving from my back smacking into the sand. Bright sunshine bursts over my tail, sending rainbow fractals of light scattering across the powdery beach. I flop back as a small wave crashes over me, clearing my mind. Without Ryan so close, I can take a breath and breathe in the salty air.

Because...whoa. What came over me? Ryan stirs something amazing in me, and we gladly give into our affections, but that was intense.

"Whoa, Luna! You okay?" A familiar voice cuts through the air, drawing my attention from the clear water where I spot Ryan transforming and changing into a human to rush to me. "Thank God you're here. Sandy said it might be a few days until someone could get to me."

Ali jogs from his spot under the shade of a palm in my direction. I inhale another deep breath, trying to get my emotions under control, still feeling Ryan's desire burning through our bond.

Flicking my tail, I slap my caudal fin against the wet sand, realizing I've beached myself. "We came as soon as we heard," I say to one of the Ocean's King's best divers.

"Are you okay?" Ryan says, coming from the waves, his eyes roving over my body for any signs of injury.

"I'm fine. Annoyed as hell but good," Ali responds.

Ryan smirks at me, because his words weren't intended for Ali. "Cool, man."

Bobbing my head, I silently answer my mate's question as he continues to watch me. I hold out my arms for him to pick me up off the sand. Ryan doesn't hesitate, scooping me up, and once again, all I can think about is snuggling with him. About being close.

Ryan cradles me in his arms and looks at Ali. "The Hurricane will be here soon. Sorry about my dad."

Ali shrugs. "Same old Wren. At least he has a new mission in life."

"I just wish it didn't interfere with our holiday," I murmur. "All I wanted was a moment to enjoy my first Winter Solstice with Ryan."

Ali steps closer, shading his eyes from the sun. "I think the chief mate might be jealous he can't follow you."

Tipping his head back, Ryan releases a loud laugh at the thought. "My dad as a merman? That's hilarious." He kisses me, showing me how he imagines his dad would look as a merman, making me laugh.

Ali grins. "I don't think it's about that. Maybe the holidays are getting to him."

Ryan whips his head back and forth, disagreeing with Ali. "He's never celebrated before. I don't see why it would matter now. If he thought they were important, he would be more perceptive now."

"He used to celebrate, you know...before your mom left." Ali scrunches his face at a memory. "It was hard on a lot of us."

"I couldn't forget."

I pout my bottom lip at Ryan's admission. He doesn't say as much, but I know if he thinks about his childhood growing up, he sometimes can't suppress the hurt he used to hold on to. Though the tides have changed for him, and he's finally getting the bond with his mom now that they can be together, it doesn't change the fact that she left him for the sea, making him believe she was dead all these years.

"Oh, Ocean," I whisper in Ryan's arms. "I've been so inconsiderate. With everything happening that thought never crossed my mind. I just thought pirates did things differently."

Ryan rests his head to mine. "Don't feel bad, Luna. I didn't even think about it either. You know how tough things are with my dad."

Even still. Ryan's doing his best to forgive Wren, but it's going to take a lot more than a few months time and some good behavior. And now this? Wren could mess up all the progress they've made to heal the relationship I want Ryan to have with his dad. Because it's important...now more than ever. This is our lineage, and Wren will be part of our legacy.

I huff a breath. "You know what? I thought I wanted to drop your dad off at the cove, but I'm pretty sure I know what I want to do."

Ryan turns his attention to me. "Find him his true love?"

I laugh, my cheeks warming at the thought. Now that's one way to tame a wild pirate. "I—"

Reaching up, Ryan touches my rosy cheek. "You love that idea way too much."

"I just hadn't thought about the possibility. I was actually going to say that maybe when we find him, we can suggest a special holiday for all of us."

"That plan is way better," he says, smirking.

"You think?"

Flicking his gaze to Ali, the two of them share a look I can't decipher. "Yeah. You don't know what love does to my dad."

I frown, trying to figure out what that is supposed to mean. "I bet it makes him a better man."

Ali kicks his boot in the sand. "It makes him something."

"I don't understand," I say. How could love make Wren anything other than a better person, especially with the merpeople way he's adapted to?

Ryan shrugs. "He just does some questionable things when..." Ryan swears without finishing his thought. He turns his attention to Ali. "You don't think that's what this is about?"

"Ah hell, maybe. I thought this might have been about the holiday, but it could definitely be," Ali says.

"It would make sense," Ryan says.

I puff a breath of air through my lips, struggling to follow along with Ryan and Ali's half conversation as they finish each other's thoughts silently. "What would make sense? I'm not following any of this."

"Wren might be in love, Luna," Ali says, finally answering my confusion.

I clap my hands, bouncing in Ryan's arms, nearly making

him drop me. "What!"

Ryan groans, adjusting my tail to hold me tighter against him. "It would make sense to why he suddenly stole the Ocean's King and has taken a great interest in reforming people to fit our life. But with who is the question? I haven't seen any mermaids around. No female crew either."

Ali whips his head back and forth. "Don't know. The guy never stops working."

"I haven't noticed anyone at all, and you know I would, Ryan," I say. "I don't think so, but now I want to make it my mission."

Ryan and Ali look at each other, and they both grimace at my words like it'd be such a bad thing to find someone for the pirate who could use a little love to make him want to better himself.

"Luna, I love you, but I'm begging of you to hold off on your desire to make my dad's dating life a mission of yours. We'll never get to dive into the sea otherwise. He'd take a lot of work. Probably all the mermen in our pod to train him for such an occasion since my dad's idea of romance is stealing the biggest diamonds or showing how tough he is."

"That would be an interesting competition," I muse.

He fake-glares at me. "Don't you dare mention it to anyone."

I laugh and pat his chest. "What will you give me for my

silence?"

"You sound like a pirate," Ryan says, smirking.

"Good."

Ryan shifts me, spinning me around to make me laugh. I catch sight of Nalani traipsing through the waves with the Hurricane dropping anchor not far from shore.

She drips water from her colorful sarong, greeting me with a brilliant smile that lights up her green eyes to match Ryan's.

"Luna, Ryan," Nalani says. "Sandy says the Ocean's King has dropped anchor not far from Pearlestria. My mate's returning to us now."

"Why don't you wait for him here, and then you can take the boat to Pearlestria and let us handle my dad?" Ryan asks. "If he's near Pearlestria, we should make it to the colony in time for the Winter Solstice celebrations."

She nods her head, still smiling at me. "Okay, if that's what you wish. But you could also let us handle it."

I shake my head. "No. I think we got it."

Ryan hugs me close. "Yeah, I think Luna won't be happy until we take care of this ourselves."

"I suppose a little extra alone time together wouldn't hurt," she says. "We'll see you in Pearlestria. I promise it'll be a grand celebration."

I can only hope.

10

TRICKY PIRATES

"DO YOU WANT THE good news or bad news," Ryan says, crossing his arms over his muscular chest.

A dozen horrifying scenarios play through my mind. Something is wrong. I could feel it even before Ryan boarded without me. Usually someone whistles or greets us, but no one has come. "Bad news."

He clenches his jaw as he smooshes his lips together like he doesn't want to have this conversation at all. "It's abandoned."

Swimming closer, I hold my hands up so he can pull me

from the water and onto the Ocean's King. "What do you mean abandoned?" Where could they have gone and why? What if someone was hurt or worse? Oh, Ocean.

Fear spills from my heart as I close my eyes and listen to the sound of the sea for any traces of pirate noise. If they were nearby in the water, I'd hear them. Pirates aren't exactly quiet, and they love their presences to be known.

"Everyone's gone. No signs of struggle or anything," Ryan says, linking his fingers through mine. He hoists me from the water and wraps his arm around my back and under the bend of my tail. "Let me show you."

Ryan carries me along the pathway circling the main deck. An eerie quiet settles through the air, and even the hum of the ocean sounds muted. What's supposed to be a magical holiday is quickly turning dark like my second favorite, only because of the candy, human holiday. Except there aren't any humans in costumes offering to feed me candy. And I won't ever forget the creepy Halloween ball thrown by the Kings. I've never seen such a sight. It was the first time being scared was actually a little fun.

"So, what's the good news?" I ask, meeting his green gaze. I need to break the silence so my mind stops trying to best me with scary things. This is nothing like the haunted ball. I knew that was sort of fake.

"It's abandoned," he repeats. How can the bad news also

be the good news?

"Ryan."

"What? It *is* a good thing. No pirates. No Dad trying to mess with the holiday." His serious gaze shifts into a smile. "No Dad in love."

I shift and peer around. "Huh? You're not making any sense."

He bites his bottom lip between his teeth in a smile. "Relax. This was all planned. We've been tricked."

I puff a breath between my lips, blowing the short strands of Ryan's hair off his forehead. "Tricked? What does that even mean?"

His smile widens, crinkling the corners of his eyes. "My dad is an evil genius."

"Are you sure? Did you check all the decks? What if everyone is dead in the cabins, and the Ocean's King has turned into a ghost ship."

Tipping his head back, Ryan releases a loud laugh, though I don't find anything about this remotely funny. I mean, he says we were tricked, but where could everyone have gone? And tricking someone isn't nice. Ryan was right about Wren being an evil genius...and a hook in my side. I have too many things to do to have been sent on a wild pirate chase.

Pushing the thought of ghouls and ghosts away, I clutch Ryan, resting my head on his shoulder. He strolls me into the saloon and out of the breezy air, setting me down on the couch with my tail and all. "This isn't funny. I need a better explanation. We were busy."

"Not really, but you were stressed. And so you know, I think you've been watching too many horror movies with Hawk. You've changed the tides, remember?" he says, kissing the pout from my lips. He might be right about the horror. Hawk refuses even to watch movies with a romantic subplot, so scary stuff it is. "You also hang around too many pirates." Again, he might be right. My mate knows me so well.

I take a breath, digging my knees into my tail. "So what now? We leave?"

Plopping down next to me, he pulls me onto his lap. "I think we should stay a while. Our crew did go through all this trouble to get us away from the cove. And Ava said that the celebration was taken care of. I know you were happy hanging out with our pod and all, but it has been a few weeks since we've been alone."

My annoyance melts away with his words. I was planning to be alone with Ryan anyway to surprise him with our life-changing news, and though Ava, Giselle, and Talia were going to plan a special celebration for Ryan after, they can still do it like tradition. "Are you sure you don't want to travel to Pearlestria? What about the fishermen."

"They're handled, remember?" he asks, running his fingers along my jawline.

"What about everything else in the colonies? I'm sure there is a lot of pre-holiday fun. I know you like to hunt."

"But I love being with you. And this was a gift to us, so we shouldn't waste it." Ryan shifts and pulls something out of his pocket. Keeping his eyes on mine, he hands me an envelope with our names scrawled across it in sloppy handwriting that looks like it says Lunu and Ryum. I'd recognize Wren's penmanship anywhere.

"Did you read it?" I ask, smiling, my fingers trembling as I touch the broken seal. I can't believe my crew went out of their way to do this.

"Yeah, and you should too." Ryan helps me pull out a card with a picture of a palm tree wrapped in rainbow lights. "My dad's lucky I agree with him and appreciate that he's finally starting to think about someone other than himself for once, or I'd drop him off at the cove for making you worry so much."

I smirk. "It's not so bad. Only a little annoying, especially with the fishermen."

"Just annoyed? You've been so stressed that you can't transform."

I nearly open my mouth to tell him what I think the real reason is, but something holds me back. I want it to be more special than just bringing it up in our casual conversation, though the thought about seeing, hearing, and feeling his reaction makes my heart pick up pace.

He notices but doesn't say anything as both our hearts thrum in quick successions. "Maybe you can try again now," he murmurs.

Ryan runs his fingers over my slippery scales for a moment before he scoops me back up into his arms to carry me to the stern. I unfold the card while he carries me to give my mind something to do besides gushing my heart out, dusting off glitter from the front of it onto my tail in the process. I carefully gather it so it doesn't blow into the sea and put it into the envelope.

"To my kids," I read out loud. "This has been one helluva year for us, and I felt kind of bad for sending ya to the cove with those asshole fishermen." I press my lips together. "At least he feels *kind of* bad."

Ryan chuckles. "This is one way to teach you to talk like a pirate. I don't think I've ever heard you cuss like that."

I laugh. Wren loves trying to enhance my vocabulary with terms our crew understands. "Don't tell the others. They'll never let me hear the end of it."

"And they'll continue to try to corrupt your pure mermaid heart."

"Pretty sure you uncorrupted everyone else's."

Setting me on the ledge of the platform, Ryan dives into

the water and comes back up, splashing a wave over my fin to wet my drying scales. Being out of water doesn't bother me like it does some others, but I can see his increased need to care for me flaring in full force, making love and appreciation nearly burst through me.

He motions at the card. "Keep reading."

"So first, I want to apologize for not consulting you. While the fishermen's acts nearly made me want to hook them on a line, I saw potential in that particular crew. It was the fourth time one of our vessels has dealt with them, and I thought it was time for a mermaid intervention." I droop my shoulders at his admission, my irritation over the situation washing back to sea. "I had good intentions but poor execution considering it's the holidays. I asked Nalani to knock some sense in me, but she don't like that shit. Never has. That's why I came up with this plan instead..."

Folding the card, I flip it over and stare at the back. There's nothing else written on it, and I re-read over the nearly illegible script again to see if I might've missed a paragraph. But then Ryan drops another card onto my lap. It's only addressed to me.

"I haven't read yours yet," Ryan says.

"Mine? Does that mean—"

He nods. "Yup. I got one too. But Dad threatened to drop anchor over Pearlestria indefinitely if I let you read it."

I scrunch my nose. "Ryan."

He chuckles. "Part of my yearning to go to sea is to have a little vacation from the Reyes Empire. I'm not risking him putting on scuba gear to try to meet us in the castle."

I giggle, his words creating a vivid picture in my mind. And it's not the first time we've talked about such a thing. I know that Carter and Ava have been giving scuba lessons to our friends and family in Azure Waters for such an adventure. When the day comes, I know Wren and some of our crew will come right alongside them in the first ever journey to a colony any human has made.

I fake-glare at him. "Fine, but then you can't read mine either."

"Sounds fair enough," he says, kissing me. "Now, go ahead and read yours and wait here. I'll be right back."

"Where are you—?"

Ryan sinks under before I can even finish my words, transforming in the water a dozen feet below. I watch him for a moment, and he waves to me without saying anything through our telepathic channel, disappearing under the yacht.

Releasing a long breath, I rip open the seal and tug out another card, this one with glittery baby Arctic seals on ice. It's a sight I love to see in person and plan to take Ryan sometime this winter if we get the chance to travel to Icilia.

My heart suddenly flutters in wild beats, and I notice a

tiny spark battling for my attention against the sun overhead. It sends a million emotions through me, bringing tears of happiness to my eyes as I realize my future merbabe reacts to my emotions and thoughts. "You like the sound of that too? An adventurer like us."

The ocean swells over my tail, begging me to return, especially because I feel the small amount of distance between me and Ryan grow a bit as he swims wherever it is he felt he needed to go.

I finally draw my attention from the ocean and back to the penguin card to keep my attention from drifting to sea.

"Luna, forgive me for probably stressing you the hell out and also for making Darren lie for me because I knew Nalani would drag me to the bottom of the ocean if I asked her, and the ex scares the shit out of me these days with her threats to be kinder. Darren I can handle." I roll my eyes. I bet he laughed the whole time writing this. "You don't have to worry. There aren't any more hostages. I needed something big enough to get you to pull yourselves away from your duties."

I groan, shaking my head.

"And I can already hear Ryan threatening to drop me off at the cove." I laugh to myself, reading the words out loud. "But I knew you wouldn't have left those damn fishermen there otherwise. Because a good captain wouldn't, and you are the best captain I've ever known. And you deserve the perfect holiday with your mate, and I'm going to assure it. So tonight, the Ocean's King is yours. You are forbidden from leaving until someone arrives to retrieve you. Enjoy your holiday. Make some new traditions with my son while you're at it. He never had much growing up."

I rest my hand on my stomach, smiling at Wren's words. Darren was right about me turning him soft-hearted. I wonder how he'll react to the news of being a grandfather and if Ryan's right about him getting the idea to go to Pearlestria. I have a feeling the colony might grow in size as my Reefaria family starts to migrate as well.

Water sloshes over my legs again, and Ryan pops through the surface. He hoists himself up next to me and surprises me with a silver fish the size of his arm. I notice a waterproof bag he hadn't been wearing before, and I tilt my head and look from it to him.

"Eat," he says. "I know you're hungry."

"What's in the bag?" I ask instead.

"I'll show you later after you eat. I can't stand hearing your stomach growling at me a moment longer." He laughs at his own words and leans in, brushing his lips to mine. "And maybe then you can try to change back. My dad left us some things to do."

Things? I know Ryan won't tell me if I ask, so I cut off a square of meat and plop it into my mouth to gather my thoughts. "I can try, but I'm pretty sure it won't work." I'm nearly certain my spark won't let me until tonight. Wren unintentionally handed me the best opportunity to change Ryan's life. It's going from better to best, and I can't wait.

"Then I won't change either for now, and the tasks can wait. We don't need the Ocean's King to start our Winter Solstice celebration. We'll start it how we started our lives together."

"You, me, and the sea?" I ask.

He smiles. "Always."

SURPRISE

RYAN'S WARM BODY CURLS around mine as we lie right in the sand, the cool waves frozen in the glittering sunset by my ocean magic. We've been lying here for hours just enjoying each other as who we are, and I'm pretty sure we'll stay here all night as the evening takes hold.

We've never slept alone on the beach like this before, and it makes my spark sing just being near Ryan, straddling the land and the sea with nothing in the world to worry about but each other.

"I want this to be a tradition," I say, turning over to face him. "Us as who we are, on the land and in the sea, together." And next year, us as our little pod, I add silently.

Ryan runs his fingers over my side. "I love the sound of that...and you."

His love floods over me, cascading from his spark to travel from his lips to mine, filling me up with everything I need in the world to survive. I roll on top of him and press my body to his to assure no more space gets between us. Ryan combs his fingers through my hair, tucking it behind my ears. He smiles, his whole face lighting in the golden sun disappearing into the horizon.

"Come on. Let's swim to the Ocean's King for a bit. There's something I want to show you," he says. "Another present arranged by my dad."

I frown, not wanting to leave this spot. I've been thinking about exactly how I'm going to surprise Ryan for hours, and I'm afraid if we move, something will interfere. "Can't it wait until morning? He's given us more than enough to last us the rest of time."

Chuckling, Ryan says, "There's something from me too."

"More? I thought tonight I could give you your gift," I say, glancing at the Ocean's King. Tucked away in our suite, I've hidden a map I've spent hours working out with all the locations I planned to take Ryan.

"My gift?" he muses. "You've given me so much already."

"Me?" I laugh. "I haven't given you anything."

He smiles. "You've given me the entire ocean, your love, your spark. An amazing time today..."

I smile with a happy sigh. "It's something small...well two things."

Leaning in, Ryan kisses me again, sending flutters through my stomach at his closeness. "Okay, but my gifts first."

I nod. "I'd like that."

Dragging the wave over us, I let it pull us into the shallows so Ryan can swim us the distance to the Ocean's King. As night descends, the massive yacht remains dark with only the rising moon to set it aglow.

Ryan flips me off his back, making me laugh through the water. He smiles and kisses me, a new excitement lighting his green eyes. I trail my fingers up his muscles, glittering with a pearlescent sheen in the ocean.

"Will you try to transform again?" he asks.

I nod and try despite knowing that my mermaid essence will cling desperately to the sea now the more I relent to my deep-seated nature. His smile turns serious as his gaze bores into mine, capturing me so I can lose myself in the green depths for the millionth time today.

"I can't do it," I whisper.

"What's holding you back?" he asks, worry scrunching his

brows. "I thought it was the stress."

I kiss him to cut off his words. "It'll be fine. I just—I need a little more time. Why don't you grab my gift for you from our suite? Second drawer under my mom's journal. No peeking."

He gives in and nods. "Okay, but swim under the boat and wait for me. I'll be right back."

Ryan arches his back and transforms. I swim him to the ladder to board the Ocean's King, and he climbs out without dressing. He grins at me from over his shoulder and shakes his cute butt in a little dance, because he knows how much being silly makes me smile. I laugh so loudly that I'm sure all the colonies in the ocean can hear me.

He waves me away, and I sink under and swim below the boat, taking in the now glowing sea around me. A school of different fish congregates closer, slowly drifting to be in touchable distance to me. Darting around my head, a small blue fish swims up to nudge my cheek. I graze my finger over its sparkly scales for a second before shooing it away. Even the marine life knows what a special occasion it is.

A strange glow lights up the surface above me, and I spin around, tempted to swim up to break through to see what's going on. Ryan dives back in the water before I even get the chance and closes the space between us, meeting me with a kiss like he's missed me.

"Close your eyes," he whispers into my mind.

I do as he asks and let him swim me away from the fish and the bottom of the Ocean's King. Ryan darts us toward the surface, and he breaches, making me screech out and laugh from the quick movements. Slowing down, he brings us back to the surface, and a breeze cools my sopping black hair.

"Are you ready?" he asks, rubbing his hands up and down my shoulders, holding me from behind.

"Yes," I say, smiling.

"Okay, then open your eyes."

I bring my hand up to my heart at the sight of the Ocean's King set aglow with thousands of twinkling colorful lights. I've never seen such a sight—a perfect blend of the land meeting the sea to create a dazzling surface that fills my spark with everything I love about the holidays.

"Wren did this?" I ask.

"He's bringing back an old tradition he gave up long ago," Ryan says.

"I love it," I say. "It's beautiful. I can't wait to tell him so."

Ryan hugs me tighter. "Hopefully you can wait a bit longer. Chief mate's orders say we must stay here. But don't worry. I have my next present to entertain you. I was hoping you could transform—"

I pout. "I'm sorry. I'm ruining everything, aren't I?"

He spins me around and shakes his head, pelting me with saltwater in the process. "Definitely not. I made a few adjustments in case."

Without letting me say anymore, Ryan hooks his arms around my waist and swims me back to the stern of the Ocean's King. On the hydraulic platform rests a blanket with a few covered plates along with the wrapped box I had asked him to retrieve for me from our suite.

Ryan helps me up, remaining in his merman form to be with me. He grins as he lifts the lids to one of the plates to show off a mound of delectable chocolate that makes my mouth water. He picks up a snowman shaped one and offers it to me to eat. "I've spent the last month collecting candy from every port we've stopped at along with a few the crew picked up for me."

I smile. "This is the best."

"I thought you could use something sweet."

"It's perfect. Thank you."

Ryan offers me another piece and immediately kisses me to taste the chocolate on my lips. I sink into him, enjoying every little thing about this moment—the glowing lights reflecting on the water, the candy that is as sweet as Ryan, how happy he is in this moment, just enjoying something as simple as feeding me and making me smile.

"This is the best Winter Solstice ever," I say.

"I was hoping you'd say that. Everything had me a bit worried."

"Well, no more worrying," I say, offering him a chocolate. "I can still feel a bit lingering inside you."

He snuggles against me, pulling my tail over his to enjoy the feeling of me in his arms. "I'll try not to. I'm just concerned about you not transforming."

Sliding my arms around his shoulders, I turn him toward me so he has to meet my gaze straight on. "There's a reason for that," I admit.

He blinks a few times, confusion puckering his brows.

Before he can ask me what the reason is, I reach over and lift up the weightless box and hold it for him to take. "But open this first."

A smile lights Ryan's face, and he kisses me again. Tearing his finger through the shiny wrapping paper, he frees the plain blue box and pops off the lid to look at the neatly folded map. He inhales a soft breath, excitement washing through him as he realizes what it is.

"Is this what I think it is?" he asks.

I nod and grin, reaching up to run my finger over his lips as they stretch into an even bigger smile. "I've planned an adventure."

"Show me. Show me." He hurries to open the map where I've circled locations and have written coordinates with a list of activities by each one. "We're going to all the colonies?"

"Yup. All seven of them," I say, smiling.

He slaps his tail on the water. "You're going to take me in the trenches?"

"Unless you're scared," I tease.

"With you? Never. You promised to always protect me in the sea." He chuckles and continues to read all the notes I left on the map. "Chase rainbows? Watch the sunrise on icebergs?"

I reach out and point to a spot on the map. "What do you think about this?"

"Get married in La Tortuga Point?" He sets the map aside and pulls me completely into his lap. Kissing me, he says, "I love it. Right where we had our first date on the glass beach. I can't wait. Seriously, you've made me the happiest guy in the universe."

"There's one more thing. I forgot to add it to the map," I say, biting my bottom lip between my teeth. "Can you get me a pen?"

Ryan scoots us both off the platform and back into the water. He transforms before me, kissing me before he clears his lungs, and I follow him back to the surface to steal his breath once again with another kiss before returning to the boat.

"Are you sure I have to get that pen?" he whispers, combing his fingers through my hair.

I nod. "It's important."

Watching me gaze at him, he rushes into the saloon and runs back to me, making me giggle in the process. He hands me the pen and dives back in the water to transform.

I trail my finger over the map and find our location to draw a heart right over the spot. Ryan emerges, excitement and wonder crashing over me. If I wasn't sitting here on the platform waiting for him, he'd probably swim a million circles to release the anticipation I build in him. I bet his merman instincts are going wild, and he doesn't even know why.

"You drew a heart over our location," he says, smiling. "The start of our adventure. I love it."

"I'm not finished," I say, grinning. "I told you I had two surprises."

Ryan intakes a sharp breath, suddenly going still next to me. A wave of emotions unlike anything I've ever experienced pours over me, sending my heart racing, set off by something I haven't done. I barely have written the number one on my list.

"Luna," he whispers.

I tilt my chin up to meet his wide green eyes, glittering in the bright moonlight overhead. His mouth hangs open, his gaze not even looking at my face or at the map. He's staring at the tiny blip of light blinking in perfect sync with our hearts a few inches below my navel and above the ridge that separates my pearlescent skin from my silver scales.

"I—" Ryan snaps his mouth shut and swallows, his Adam's apple bobbing in his throat. "Is that? Are you?"

Reaching out, I touch his chin to get him to look at me. "Surprise."

"Really?"

I laugh and grab the map to finish writing number one on the list of things to do on our adventure.

"Do you remember what you told me at our coupling ceremony?" I ask.

"That the sea told me it wanted us to help it flourish," he says, his shock turning into a smile. "So we can make a better world together."

"For our future," I say.

Ryan grins and grazes his fingers across the tiny blip of light on my stomach. "Oh, Ocean. This is incredible. The best. I love you, Luna. And I—" He flings his arms around me and dives me into the sea with him. He sinks down, running his fingers from my spark to the new one now blinking as fast as his—as mine. A piece of the essence we share will now grow into something made from our love. The light glows for us, reminding us of what our amazing future holds.

Ryan presses his cheek over the tiny spark without saying anything, but his emotions crash into me with so much love— for me, for our merbabe, for our futures together. Our adventure.

"I promise you that this adventure of ours will be the best," I say, combing my fingers through his hair. "Happy Winter Solstice, Ryan."

"It's everything I've imagined already," he whispers. "And so much more. I can't wait to meet her and hold her. Teach her everything."

"Her?" I ask.

He flicks his tail, sliding up to face me. "Yeah. I'm nearly certain. I don't know how, but I just know."

I laugh and hug him. "You really are a healer."

"And you're the most magical being in all the universe." Ryan lowers himself in the water to kiss my stomach. "I bet you will be, too. Part princess, part pirate. "

"Made from love and magic."

He smiles. "The best parts of us."

"The very best."

12

BEST HOLIDAY EVER

A LOUD LAUGH SOUNDS through the air, stirring me awake from Ryan's arms. My magic hold on the sea breaks on the wave, sending it over our heads, and I inhale a breath of saltwater. My body revolts from the action, and I cough and spit, my chest heaving. I realize I'm no longer in my mermaid form, but I don't remember transforming.

Ryan hooks his arm around me and tugs me back to the beach, sliding onto the sand in his merman form. Turning me over, he pats my back until my lungs get enough air to stop me from coughing.

"You transformed," he says, inspecting me inch by inch. "By accident?"

Now that he knows I'm expecting, he'll surely coddle me even more. Mermen are already protective. I can just imagine things now. It might be a good thing I've planned a new adventure for us in the sea considering our crew doesn't always think before they act.

"Yeah, but this is a good thing," I say, touching his cheek. "I was worried that I'd be stuck until...our merbabe arrives and learns to transform herself. And if she's anything like me—"

"She's going to be amazing." Ryan snuggles against me, sending my heart racing. "I just want to figure out why you changed now. I haven't."

Another burst of laughter cuts through the air, drawing my attention away from Ryan. "It's because of Talia," I say, catching sight of Tide breaching with her from the water again as they make their way to the Ocean's King. "She was worried that she'd lose me to the sea, and I bet yesterday and my inability to change didn't help, but I think I wasn't able to because, well, I think my body wanted nothing more than to tell you and wasn't going to relent until I did."

"Luna! Ryan!" Talia's voice rips through the air as she calls our names.

I spot her standing on the Ocean's King, waving her

hands over her head. Ryan releases a soft breath against my shoulder and scoots us back to the water, adjusting me on his back while not giving me a chance to transform. He swims us to the Ocean's King in one of my breaths, and Talia holds up a towel for me.

Talia engulfs me into a hug. "You've transformed again. I was worried. I mean, I know it's not the end of the world, but...have you told Ryan?" Her words come out a whisper.

"Last night."

"Perfect!" she shrieks. She tackles Ryan as he starts to climb up the ladder, and they both fall overboard. My heart practically bursts watching the two of them hug. She kisses both of his cheeks, squishing his face and making him laugh.

A wave of water cascades over me next, and Tide hops aboard in his merman form and drops a huge red fish right onto the deck next to me. "Lia told me the magnificent news." Surprises are hard to keep secret, but especially in the sea where information passes quickly. "You'll be an amazing mom, Princess Luna."

I hug Tide once more and bite right into the fish he brought to show him my appreciation. Ryan helps Talia back onto the boat, and he comes to my side with only a towel wrapped around his hips. I offer him a piece of the fish, which he eats from my fingers before kissing the tips.

"So, is everything okay?" I ask, bumping my shoulder to

Talia. "Please don't tell me something else has happened."

"Our pod has it handled. We're only here to assure you return to Pearlestria," she says. "Though, I can tell them you're still celebrating with Ryan if you want me to. I wouldn't blame you. The surface is quite packed."

"It is?" I ask.

Talia nods. "I can't tell you any more because Wren threatened—"

I glare. "He better—"

She laughs. "He threatened to encourage the pirates to adapt to the merpeople social norms, and I know it's not a big deal to you, but I deal with enough asshole pirates that I don't care to add their asses to the mix as well."

"Remind me to teach you about focused vision," I say. "Selective sight."

"Oh, please do," she says, hugging me tight. "In case."

Ryan and Tide insist Talia and I hang out and just enjoy the journey to Pearlestria. I had planned on swimming, but Ryan said bringing the Ocean's King was a must, and Wren would have a coronary if we just left it anchored here for another day. It might be my ship, but it means a million times more to him than it does me. That thought alone proves how sweet his gesture was to offer it to me and Ryan for the start of our new holiday traditions.

The orange glow of the sun fades with the oncoming

night. A few whistles sound through the air, but I don't get a chance to get up from the couch, where Talia and I have been watching the only Christmas movie in Wren's collection about a giant elf who likes holidays as much as me. Giselle and Ava rush into the saloon, dripping water all over the place. They both nearly attack me in the form of hugs and kisses, petting my hair, drenching my dress.

"Happy Winter Solstice!" they both shout in unison and then laugh together.

They tug me and Talia to our feet, and practically drag us to the door. Ava twirls behind me and covers my eyes with her hands. Giselle and Talia can't stop giggling and laughing as they skip their way to wherever Ava nudges me. She tells me to keep my eyes closed, and steps away from me.

I sense Ryan immediately, my heart thumping hard enough to try to throw itself at him, and then butterflies swirl in my stomach.

"Oh, whoa," Ava whispers under her breath. "Carter, I wish you could see. It's so cute."

She doesn't have to be specific for me to know she's talking about the tiny spark flickering in my stomach, reacting to my emotions of being near Ryan. I almost tell her that Carter will get his chance with her, but she murmurs again under her breath, I keep the thought to myself.

"Careful, Aves," he whispers back to her. "I can feel your

heart drifting to sea, and you know how excited I'd be to follow you."

She giggles without saying anything.

I sigh a happy breath.

"I swear it better not be contagious," Giselle murmurs, making both me and Ava laugh.

Warm fingers link through mine, and I pull Ryan's hand up to kiss his fingers, holding them against my cheek. A horn blares nearby, and I bounce on my feet, dying to open my eyes to see what all the commotion is about.

Another horn beeps through the air, and then someone whistles.

"I know we were planning to throw a small celebration last night," Ava says.

"But then Wren had to interfere, but luckily his gift to you fit perfectly with our plan."

Ava laughs. "And he doesn't even know it."

Ryan groans. "Do we have to tell him?"

I squeeze his hand. "Even if he takes up the adventure to scuba dive into Pearlestria, we'll be fine."

He pulls me close, wrapping me in a hug. "We'll be better than fine."

Water sloshes over our feet, drawing our attention from each other, though I keep my eyes closed. The familiar sound of heavy boots tapping on the deck resonates nearby, and then

Wren clears his throat.

"Ryan, Luna," the old pirate king says. "I never thought life could be like this, and I have to say, it's way damn better than I used to run things. You two reminded me what I loved about the ocean. You've reminded me that it's more than just about me. So, I wanted to thank you with an old tradition that my dad used to do."

"We're not deck wrestling, are we?" Ryan asks.

Wren laughs.

"And you didn't steal anything, right?" he adds.

"I'll show you the damn receipts if that makes you happy," Wren barks a loud laugh. "You're never going to let me live those things down, are you?"

"Never," Ryan says, teasingly. "And I'll make sure my daughter never does either."

Absolute silence greets us, and I snap my eyes open. I can't help it. I didn't hear the ocean swell up to knock Wren under, but his new quietness makes me want to check that he still stands before us just in case.

"Surprise!" Over a thousand voices ring through the air at once, startling Wren. He steps back and falls right into the water and into the muscular arms of Sailor, who laughs and kisses his cheek.

I draw my eyes to the scene in front of me, holding Ryan's hand to my flickering spark as I take in the colorful lights reflecting on the water like rainbows cutting across the surface. Our entire fleet is present, each of our vessels decorated for the festivities. All of the colonies have gathered as well, packed on the surface just like Talia had said.

Ava raises her hands next to me, pulling dozens of glittering water orbs from the sea to sparkle through the air along with the rainbow lights. I've never seen such a magnificent sight as the land and sea come together to meet on the surface to celebrate not only a festive occasion, but to also celebrate the start of my and Ryan's new journey in life.

"Happy Winter Solstice!" Ava shouts, quieting the crowd the best she can. "We're gathered here above the most magical place in all the seas to celebrate the longest night of the year under the light of the moon. Here we celebrate the union of our pods and colonies, of families from ashore and on the surface with love and happiness and a fresh beginning as we enter a new season in our lives."

"We've also gathered here to celebrate the start of a new adventure as merpeople and humans, to strengthen our bonds to create an amazing future for everyone," I say, continuing the speech with a few adjustments of my own.

Ryan hugs me from behind, and I slowly raise the water to bring Wren, who Sailor helped aboard a glowing tender boat with my dad and Dara, Nalani and Sandy, and Darren closer to me to look them straight in the eyes. Without my mom needing even to be here, I feel her magic rippling through the air and water and can see and feel her love in every molecule and bubble, in every spark beating with excited anticipation.

Ava smiles and hugs her arms around the both of us. "Including the next princess of Pearlestria, daughter of Princess Luna Torres-Lazaro-Reyes and Prince Ryan Reyes, the reigning king and queen of the Reyes Empire."

Cheers erupt through the air, and Ryan lifts me up to jump us into the water. We transform together and get passed to our pod waiting for us. I've never felt so much love and joy in my life, being with a pod bigger than I could have ever imagined.

"A grandpa," Wren says, hugging me. "Our little princess will be the toughest in all the seas."

"With the kindest heart," Nalani says, bumping her shoulder to his.

"Well loved," Dad says, taking me into his arms. "A warrior in the making."

"With the most amazing future ahead. Your mom would be so proud," Darren says, his eyes glassing over. "I'm proud."

Ryan hugs me again, kissing me tenderly on the lips. "And I'm so in love. I've never felt so complete. You, me, and..."

"What about Marina Celestiana?" I ask. "After my great-grandmer and mom."

Ryan nods with a smile. "It's perfect. You're perfect."

I can't stop smiling. Surely my cheeks will never recover. "And you're my everything. You, me, Marina, our pod, the ocean, the land, the surface."

"You, me, and the world," Ryan says.

I nod. "Forever."

EPILOGUE

A MERMAZING FUTURE

"SMILE, LUNA," RYAN SAYS, holding up his phone to snap a picture.

A white seal pup jumps onto my lap, surprising me, and I tip my head back, releasing a loud laugh. It snuggles close, and I motion for Ryan to take another picture. A wave knocks into Ryan, jostling him, and he accidentally drops his phone. It slides across the ice right toward the edge to plummet into the water.

Waving my hand, I summon a wave of water, and it freezes immediately, locking Ryan's phone in place. Ryan dives off the ledge, choosing to swim to the frozen wave instead of slide across the ice.

"Good catch," he says, smiling at me, his black hair turning white with frost. "Gi threatened to hunt us down if we don't send enough pictures, and I'm afraid she'll never give us another minute alone until...maybe until Marina couples."

"You're probably right," I say with a smile. "But that's what soul sister's do. I even think she might be coming around to the whole—"

"You better not say coming around to the whole make the seas flourish thing," Giselle says into my mind.

The water rises before us and out pops Giselle and Ava. Sun and Carter soon follow, and a few of the lazy arctic seals stir from their spots, their interests piqued by the arrival of more mermaids. The seal pup jumps from my arms and nearly sinks Giselle under. She laughs and snuggles it before it dives to Ava.

Carter flicks his tail and hoists Ava and the pup up on the ice next to me. Giselle breaches herself, smiling at Sun as he puffs his chest out in pride, always loving every minute of Giselle's independence.

"What are you all doing here? Is everything okay?" I ask.

Ryan swims back to me and rests his arms on my tail. "Don't answer any of her questions."

Giselle flicks her tail, splashing water at him. "Do we need a good reason to interrupt your adventure?"

I shake my head. "No, but—"

She smiles and hugs me. "Good. We're only here because we've missed you all."

It's only been a few weeks since Ryan and I decided to migrate through the seas to celebrate our coupling and new journey in life, and I can already feel the shift in the world. I swear the rainbows shine more vibrantly, the sunsets are always the color of cotton candy to assure calm waters, and as for my pod? We're closer than ever. Just a few days ago Nalani and Sandy met us to check in with us in Icilia.

"And we've missed you." I touch my stomach, the small blip of light flickering to speed up both mine and Ryan's sparks. "Especially Marina."

"Aw, I love her so much already," Giselle says, covering my hand with hers. "Sun promised to build us a summer home in Pearlestria."

"It'll be perfect for the fall as well, my love. We can have our weekend getaway while you're in school," Sun says.

She groans, dramatically sighing. "I don't even want to think about that now. I mean, I'm going to be an aunt. That's a huge deal."

Sun chuckles. "While that's true, my warrior princess, you promised your mom, and I promised her I wouldn't take you to sea so soon."

"School first, mermaid later," she mutters.

"There are plenty of online classes," Carter says.

"It's not about that. It's about keeping up with our life," she complains. "Galas and socializing. All the fundraising."

Sun kisses her. "And you're making our world even more beautiful."

I beam a smile, soaking in all of their love and excitement. Ryan coaxes me from the ice and into his arms, holding me against him like too much time has passed since we've cuddled.

Giselle jumps from her spot and into Sun's arms. "God, I didn't think you guys could love each other any more than you already do. It's intense...but weirdly satisfying."

"Just wait until you officially couple, Gi," Ava says. "Maybe in the spring? Two weddings and a coupling?"

I clap my hands. "Yes! It's the perfect time. The Spring Equinox would be amazing."

Giselle holds her hands up. "Whoa, slow your waves. I haven't been formally asked."

Ryan, Carter, and Sun all give each other a look, having an obvious merman-to-merman conversation that leaves the rest of us out. But none of us mermaids mind.

Pressing my lips together, I suppress my smile. "Yet."

"Yet," Giselle repeats. "Plus, coupling might make that whole merbabe thing contagious."

I laugh. "You're silly."

She rolls her eyes, tossing her hair over her shoulder. "Whatever. I don't have anything to worry about. If anything, it's our BFF queen mermaid." Giselle thinks the thought only to me, and I glance at Ava.

She hugs Carter, resting her head on his shoulder, and without even having to feel her emotions, I know she drifts deeper into the sea.

I nod at Giselle. "You're right."

"What's Giselle right about?" Ava asks.

I realize that everyone's staring at me and Giselle because I opened up my telepathic channel to all of them. Blush heats my face, and I touch my hands to my stomach, leaning back into Ryan.

"That you're next," I say, my smile widening.

She and Carter share a look, a wave of undeniable love crossing their faces at even the thought.

"To make the seas flourish."

Ava shakes her head and laughs before kissing Carter. "I guess we'll see, huh?" she says, flicking her tail to swim the two of them away. "But until then, let's just enjoy this adventure."

I hug my arms around Ryan, pressing my whole body to his, just feeling a million amazing emotions pass between us. Giselle squeals out through the water as Sun flies them past us to start a race with Carter. Ryan jets us to catch up, and I smile against his lips.

"This is all I've ever wanted, you know," Ryan says to me, swimming us ahead.

I touch his cheek, peering into his green eyes. "And I promise it'll always be this way."

"And I plan to enjoy every second of it...and you."

I kiss him. "Good, because that's all I've ever wanted."

~The End~

Thank you so much for reading *Holiday Waters*! I hope you loved Luna and Ryan's story as much as I loved writing it. To stay up-to-date on future Luna and Ryan stories and other new releases, sign up for Ginna's newsletter. You can also follow her on Amazon or Bookbub.

OTHER YOUNG ADULT SERIES BY GINNA MORAN

PARANORMAL

Destined for Dreams Series
Demon Within Series
Finding Nate Series
Going Ghostly Series
Spark of Life Series
When Souls Collide Series
Demon Watcher Series
Call of the Ocean Series

REVERSE HAREM

The Divine Vampire Heirs Series

CONTEMPORARY

Falling into Fame Series
Life After Lila

ABOUT GINNA MORAN

GINNA MORAN IS a writer from sunny Southern California. She started writing poetry as a teenager in a spiral notebook that she still has tucked away on her desk today. Her love of writing grew after she graduated high school, and she completed her first unpublished manuscript at age eighteen.

When she realized her love of writing was her life's passion, she studied literature at Mira Costa College in Northern San Diego. Besides writing novels, she was senior editor, content manager, and image coordinator for Crescent House Publishing Inc. for four years.

Aside from Ginna's professional life, she enjoys binge watching television shows, playing pretend with her daughter, and cuddling with her dogs. Some of her favorite things include chocolate, anything that glitters, cheesy jokes, and organizing her bookshelf.

Ginna Moran loves to hear from her readers so visit her online at www.GinnaMoran.com. You can also find her on

Facebook, Twitter, Instagram, and Snapchat. To stay up-to-date on new releases, sign up to her newsletter. You'll not only get exclusive access to extra stories, but you'll be able to participate in monthly giveaways!

Ginna Moran is currently hard at work on her next novel.

www.ingramcontent.com/pod-product-compliance
Lightning Source LLC
Chambersburg PA
CBHW032028180726
48284CB00008B/2524